PARKING LOT OF TERROR!

Rat lunches! thought Melvinge. *Caught way outside the Gabovnikon, and without my bug spray!* He shouldn't have taken Harlan outside for a walk—this was definitely a low-rent section of the parking lot, just off the Interstate.

The lead gypsy—he looked like a pirate with a clown's fashion sense—grunted and traded comments with his companions in their gypsy language, Goulash-ese. The gypsies laughed uproariously, then turned their avocado-stained teeth framed in nasty grins back to Melvinge and Harlan.

"Den, my leetle friend . . . you will have some *moneee* to lend to us, yes?"

"You see," said another of the gypsies. "We are the Official Sleeze-e Interstate Toll Collectors. We normally only take spare change, but you are de lucky One Thousandth Customer!"

"Yes," said another. "You get to give us *all* your moneee!"

"Ohhh ohhh . . ." Melvinge cried. "You're . . . I.R.S.!"

"Interstate Robbers Supreme!" yapped Harlan.

DANIEL M. PINKWATER'S

1

MELVINGE OF THE MEGAVERSE

NIGHT OF THE LIVING SHARK!

BY DAVID BISCHOFF

A GLC Book

ACE BOOKS, NEW YORK

Night of the Living Shark! is an original publication of The Berkley Publishing Group. This work has never appeared before in book form.

An Ace Book/published by arrangement with General Licensing Company, Inc.

PRINTING HISTORY
Ace edition / October 1991

A GLC BOOK

Daniel M. Pinkwater's Melvinge of the Megaverse is a trademark of General Licensing Company, Inc.
Cover and logo design by Steve Brenickmeyer.
Cover art by Steve Fastner and Rich Larson.

ISBN: 0-441-57482-3

Ace Books are published by The Berkley Publishing Group,
200 Madison Avenue, New York, NY 10016.
The name "Ace" and the "A" logo
are trademarks belonging to Charter Communications, Inc.

PRINTED IN THE UNITED STATES OF AMERICA

10 9 8 7 6 5 4 3 2 1

For the Stones Family—
Tad, Lisa, Brenna,
Chris and Zach

Introduction

The Megaverse Mall is the largest shopping mall ever conceived. Centrally located in Time, Space, and the Other (more about the Other in the book itself!) off the Interstate, the Megaverse Mall serves the needs of uncounted life forms from every world and time.

The parking has accommodation for over 178,000,000 vehicles of every description. And there are generally 336,000,000 vehicles cruising for a space.

The average visit to the Megaverse Mall lasts three to four lifetimes, the first of which is spent looking for a parking place, and the last looking for that place again after visiting the Mall. Most visitors never see the Mall, having been distracted by one of the improvised satellite malls, containing only a few thousand emporia. These gypsy malls, erected without permission by freebooters, are demolished by the Megaverse Management Company when they are discovered—generally after thirty or forty years of profitable operation.

Some simple souls go home having seen one of these imposter malls, believing they've seen THE Mall. ("See one mall, you've seen The Mall," is a pun incomprehensible to most, which has appeared on bumper stickers for millennia.)

The actual Megaverse Mall is often taken for the Christian heaven. You can get jeans there. There's a cookie shop. A Radio Shack, of course. And a place where you can get sausage products and cheese. And Cinema 100,000.

After perhaps four lifetimes, a family having come to the Mall may make to depart with its newly acquired lava light, waterbed, designer jeans, plastic shoes, rock 'n' roll records—some happy, some sad, some newborn, some dead—but always vowing to come again to the Greatest Mall in Creation.™

In the parking lot, murder is common, as is accidental death arising from one life form failing to recognize other life forms as such. Common victims are Germ-people and Pebble-people—and of course Parking-space men are crushed to death in great numbers.

There are periodic raids by pirates and predators (which events are merely rumors in those parts of the parking lot where they are not happening), likewise, wars, famines, hurricanes, and plagues.

Because the Megaverse Mall attracts people from not only different places, but also from different times—all times—it's possible that one might meet one's ancestors, and also one's descendents. It's statistically unlikely that one will meet anybody one knows there—yet people do (like in New York City). The complementary theory is that if one were to stay there long enough one would meet everybody there is or ever was or will be, because sooner or later everybody goes there, even people who claim they don't like it.

The parking lot is the scene of all the action. It has the aspect of a gigantic fair or encampment. Some of the flavor can be inferred from the following paraphrase from *Slaves of Spiegel*:

Androids, gleptoids, intelligent robots, werewolves, insubstantial thoughtforms, mineral-creatures, astral jellyfish, giant Manx cats, and the clown-men of Noffo are present. There are also musicians and actors, jugglers and acrobats, fortune-tellers and wise men, dancers and swindlers. There are space doctors tending to the ills of every creature from every world.

3

There are barbers who charge according to how many hairs the customer has, and others who charge according to how many heads.

Tents and prefabricated buildings have been erected. Itinerant restarauteurs have set up many sausage stands, pizza parlors, soda fountains, bakeries, candy shops, deep-fried chopped-liver wagons, mayonnaise carts, and bagel factories.

Pilgrims and shoppers *cum* merrymakers walk, crawl, hop, slither, fly, and float about, all day and all night, enjoying the many pleasant spectacles. There are roast goose jugglers, meteor swallowers, monsters able to turn themselves inside out, many-mouthed musicians who can play fifteen horns at once, pseudo-octopusian Fandango dancers, and whistlers from Glintnil. There are mixed beast races, wrestling matches against giant slothoids from Neptune, six-dimensional chess games, screaming contests, and the knocking down of three milk bottles with a baseball.

Spontaneous triumphs and parades are common. Also entertainments sponsored by local warlords and politicians. Typically, they begin with gleptillian musicians, glepts, pseudo-glepts and gleptiles from the galaxy of Twilbstein. Each gleptoid is capable of producing the sound for a full ninety-piece symphony orchestra from within his own body. A phalanx of a hundred such musicians, wearing gleptizoidal helmets, might sound the fanfare announcing a spectacle.

Next might come rank upon rank of Freddians. Known for their sweetness, these adorable inhabitants of the planet Fred distribute bouquets of space orchids, onions, and zitzkisberries to the insanely happy crowd, and put everybody in an even better mood—if that is possible.

Giant ducks from a planet of unknown origin are led through the makeshift streets, each duck held by a stout chain in the hands of a powerful Spiegelian pirate. The crowds cheer, the ducks snarl and hiss. The pirate duck-handlers control the fearsome beasts.

A succession of strange and amusing animals is led before the crowd. Fluorescent lizards, singing walruses, lighter-than-air bears, wombats (both wild and domesticated)—these and many other rare zoological specimens are presented to the enthralled spectators.

Next come famous people: foreign dignitaries, ambassadors from other worlds, heroes, celebrities, newscasters, athletes, and interplanetary rock stars.

Here is Rolzup, the Martian High Commissioner, a great favorite of the crowd. Here is the Ugly Bug Band, a famous rock group of which all the members are ugly bugs. Here is Dr. Kissinger, the reincarnated Attila the Hun, the Three Stooges, and the ghostly form of Alexander the Great.

If the spectacle is by way of celebration of a victory in war, or the arrival of a band of pirates, there may be an exposition of plunder and captives.

That's why everyone's going to the Megaverse Mall.

For now, let's tune in on a certain Time, Space, and the Other vehicle, and listen as the story unfolds. . . .

Chapter One

Let me tell you the tale of a guy named Melvinge,
Oi! It's a great and wondrous science-fractional
    story!
If the jokes and the Yiddish words don't make
    you cringe,
You're in for an adventure of wacky, actionful
    glory!

—Blind Grapefruit

In the Beginning there was the Interstate.

At the End there was the Interstate.

In the Middle there was the Megaverse Mall.

And somewhere on the outskirts of this Mall, in one of the parking lots with cheap rates, there was this guy named Melvinge and his dog Harlan.

Melvinge was a mild young fellow with a ready smile, limp blond hair, and a constant craving for candied kumquats. He was the sort of guy who'd be into computers and carry pens and pencils in a Thriftee-Save plastic pocket protector if he lived on the planet Earth (which occupies one of the lesser satellite parking lots and is deliberately kept in the dark about the

7

existence of the Megaverse for fear of the Mall Children being exposed to the Wrong Element). However, Melvinge did not live on Earth and so he looked much different.

Melvinge had a round nose and round eyes and a round belly from eating too many candied kumquats. He wore a beanie and a striped shirt. We poor mortals should envy Melvinge because, unlike so many of us, Melvinge had a Purpose in Life. He had a Noble Goal, a Glorious Quest.

He wanted to find the Megaverse Mall because he needed a new pair of squash shoes. (Not tennis shoes. Only the most objectional Earth-type folks in the universe wore tennis shoes. No, squash shoes, made from real summer squashes.)

He also had a faithful dog. (Well, sort of faithful. He faithfully ate most everything Melvinge gave him. Except candied kumquats.)

The dog's name was Harlan and he really wasn't your average dog since he was kinda humanoid, but we can explain that later because it's more complicated than Neo-Sub-Bipartisan Howie Mendelian genetics.

Together, Melvinge and Harlan travelled in the Grabovnikon, a Time, Space, and the Other machine that would have caused H. G. Wells, Jules Verne, and the entirety of NASA massive cases of heartburn. The Grabovnikon was an invention of Melvinge's father, Ratner, which utilized physics-bending engines. Its ultra-hi-tech beyond-the-future power source (radio-active Snickers bars) just happened to be fitted inside the largest craft Ratner could find in his neighborhood junkyard: a Winnebago Recreational Vehicle, complete with a "Spending Our Children's Inheritance" bumper sticker.

Ah, the wonders of technology! After all (as Ratner always said, looking with wonder at the advances of Megaversal Technology), this was The Day After Yesterday! Nothing was impossible—except maybe finding a decent knish at a comfort station. And, of course, reasonably priced parking.

So together Melvinge and Harlan sought the Megaverse Mall, dodging speed traps and time troopers and the Fun Police. Together they wended their way through the trials and tribulations of the multitudinous parking lots that surrounded the Mall for light-years all around. Occasionally they encountered False Malls and had to resist the allure of shoddy merchandise and sidewalk sales and the odd Valley Girl who wanted to neck with Melvinge, "Fer sure!"

"Son," Ratner had told him, "when you see the Megaverse Mall, you'll have no doubt that it's the One True Mall!"

"Why, father?" Melvinge had said. "How?"

"Why, the 'One True Bloomingdale's' exhibit, of course, transplanted brick by brick from the heart of Manhattan!"

Where Melvinge came from and the reason he wanted to go to the Mall and get those (dried) squash shoes will come later. Right now, I, your Temporary Narrator, David Bischoff, would like to mention that at this very moment (or as close as trans-Springsteen time/space/other physics will permit) our hero and his dog are being accosted near a rutabaga-soda vending machine by suspicious-looking gypsies with *Elvis Lives in My Basement* tattoos on their earlobes.

"Hey guy," said the Gypsy Leader of the Pack, thumbing off a boom box that had been playing Pat Boone Golden Moldies. "You comin' from the Big M, goin' to the Big M—" He spat out a wad of avocado gum juice—"or are you just Hangin' Out?"

The Pack hung back, their colorful gypsy clothes rippling in the parking lot breeze, their earrings and jewelry jangling like five-and-dime windchimes. Their clodhoppered feet still tapped lugubriously to "Don't Step on My Blue Suede Shoes."

Rat lunches! thought Melvinge. *Caught way outside the Grabovnikon, and without my bug spray!* He shouldn't have taken Harlan outside for a walk—this was definitely a low-rent section of parking lot, just off the Interstate. He shouldn't have taken that shoddy ramp marked HOBOKEN REJECTS. He should have just pulled off to the side, like most smart travellers in questionable parts of the Megaverse did. Instead, here he was staring down the Bela Lugosi Fan Club.

"Uh, uh, uh," he said, futtering as he always did when he got scared or nervous. Most people *stuttered* when they got nervous. Melvinge *futtered*. He got caught on vowels, not consonants.

The answer, of course, was that Melvinge was headed *to* the Megaverse Mall. The reason was, of course, to get those new shoes, but he'd been heading *to* the Mall even before he realized he'd needed the new shoes. It just seemed like *everybody* was either going to the Mall, coming *from* the Mall—or (if you were lucky) actually shopping *at* the Mall. Like his pop, Ratner the itinerant funeral-director, said, "You're born, you live, you die— and if you're lucky, you get a nice couple scoops of Eggplant Tofutti with sprinkles at the Megaverse Mall while you're young enough to enjoy 'em!"

Harlan knew Melvinge's answer, of course, and he supplied it. "We're going *to* the Mall, of course, you garlic galoomphers! Whadda ya think we are—pikers?!"

The lead gypsy—who looked like a pirate with a clown's fashion sense—grunted and traded comments with his companions in their gypsy language, Goulash-ese. The gypsies laughed uproariously, then turned their avocado-stained teeth framed in nasty grins back to Melvinge and Harlan.

"Den, my leetle friend . . . you will have some *moneeeee* to lend to us, yes?" He held out a large, hairy hand, bald palm upwards. It looked like a launching pad for a Flea Air Force squadron.

"You see," said another of the gypsies. "We are the Official Sleeze-E Interstate Toll Collectors. We normally only take spare change, you are de lucky One Thousandth Customer!"

"Yes," said another. "You get to give us *all* your moneee!"

"Ohhh ohhhh . . . Yooooou're . . . I.R.S.!" Melvinge futtered.

"Interstate Robbers Supreme!" yapped Harlan, wagging his half-humanoid, half-dogoid tail.

"Yesss . . ." said the leader. "And here are 1042 forms to fill out. . . ." He pulled out a large Tennessee Slugger baseball bat from behind him.

"Yes—and here are some pens!"

The others pulled out gigantic Girl Scout knives . . . and they didn't want to play mumble-ty-peg.

Melvinge ceased futtering. He simply could not speak. This was all Harlan's fault. The creature was absolutely full of problems in this incarnation. Perhaps, thought Melvinge, Harlan will now solve this terrible problem by pulling some kind of trick out of his metaphorical hat.

The only trick that Harlan pulled was a speedy about-face, a burst of speed, and a *yip-yip-yip* back to the hulking bulking form of the Grabovnikon a hundred yards away . . . abandoning his master, poor Melvinge, to a sorry fate.

"Your money, pork-rind breath!" The gypsies twirled their knives. "Or are we going to have to go *prospecting* for it?"

Now in his youth, back in Fozz (you take a right at Oz, go about a mile down to Lemuria and then hang a right past Moo—the lost continent of cows), Melvinge had taken lessons in the marital arts. Husbands and wives fight constantly in Fozz, and both have developed separate and distinct schools of self-defense— men generally using "moo goo gai pan" and women "moo she" (of course). As "moo she" usually involves barbecued pork, pancakes, and rolling pins, and as Melvinge had none of these weapons, he utilized "moo goo gai pan" which needs only the hands, the head, the feet, and a shaker of monosodium glutamate.

"Ha . . . aaa . . . aaa . . . aaaa!" he futtered, taking out the MSG (marital arts mace) and tossing it into the eyes of his attackers. He then proceeded to do his version of the "Can Can Meets Sugar Ray Leonard," striking the gypsies a number of times. He clearly surprised them with his fight, unsuspected in someone so young, so timid-looking, and so vulnerable.

Whak!

Zonk!

Quack!

Quack? That particular sound took Melvinge right out of the zen ramen-noodle trance he had built up, throwing him off balance entirely.

One boink on the kisser by a gypsy fist, and Melvinge, Quester for the Megaverse Mall, was down for the count.

The gypsies wiped the MSG out of their eyes (which really smarts—don't try it) and then carted Melvinge back to the glowing fires and bubbling pots and billowing tents of the gypsy encampment. . . . And back to the Gypsy Queen, Magda Novaleen, to have her plunder not merely his piggy bank, but his mind, and maybe play a game of mah-jongg for funsies.

This unconscious period in our hero's life is quite unfortunate and yes, quite *dangerous* for him. . . .

And this series of Daniel Pinkwater books may well stop before it really even gets going.

However, frankly, *I'm* pleased, because this gives me a chance to push aside my marital martial arts books, my MSG shaker, my copies of *Fat Men from Outer Space, Lizard Music,* and the *1949 Book of Baseball Statistics* and present not just the Big Picture, but . . .

The MEG PICTURE!

Chapter Two

More Bizarre Stuff About the Mall

Sorry about the rude imposition,
We've gotta have some crude exposition!
                                   —Blind Grapefruit

Behold (blare of trumpets, rat-tat-tat of snare drums, hosannas of the Moronic Tubercular Choirbcys . . .)—

The Meg-Universal Mall!

Folks, you ain't gonna see this in pictures, so don't skip this section and go to your library and bother that geeky old guy in glasses behind the desk.

No, the Meg-Universal Mall is simply too big for mere two-dimensional pictures to encompass. (And 3-D—forget it! We're talking MAMMOTH here, boyo!)

How big?

Big as . . . big as . . . oh goodness, my mind is boggling at the very concept! (Even seen a mind boggle? Not a pretty sight. Ever see a corn-chip bugle like Escher gone bananas? That's a close approximation.)

Let's just say that it's the largest shopping mall ever conceived and it's smack-dab right in the middle of, like, the whole (and we're talking everything-AND-the-kitchen-sink here) *Cosmos*.

Blind Grapefruit, the travelling bard, prophet, and Fuller Brush Salesman, had been on a jag one day early in Melvinge's life, singing the praises yet again of the Megaverse Mall—or "where all the Soft Pretzels go to go stale, where brown M and M's are outlawed except in the Out-Mall by the men's room, and where a bloke can still get a decent egg cream!" and Melvinge had stopped him. This was a time when he, his father Ratner, his mother Malovia, and their dog Fafner (now Harlan) had lived so happily and contently in a place where the Interstate was just a dull roar south of Boise, Oh-ho-ho and the Mall was just a myth-understanding.

"Tell me about the Meg-Universal Mule, Blind Grapefruit. But could you try not to rhyme this time. Rhymes make me break out."

"That's *Mall*, sunny boy," the old bluesbrother said. "And my special magic eightball tells me that it is your destiny!" Blind Grapefruit put down his womandolin (a mandolin that is much more pleasant to hold), picked up young

Melvinge, and placed him on one of his three available knees (Blind Grapefruit was one of the Poor and Kneedy).

"My destiny!"

"Yes, Melvinge. For one day when you grow up, you will make a quest!"

"How do you know that, Blind Grapefruit?"

Blind Grapefruit scratched his bald head. "Don't rightly know, son. To hang out and check out the babes? Try me and the eightball later. Anyway, that there Interstate out there . . ."

"You mean Root 69?"

"Yeah, Root 69 is the part of the Freeway that passes here. You get on the Interstate and you travel. All roads may lead to Rome, Pennsylvania, sonny boy. But all Interstates lead to the Mall."

"Does God live there?"

"Don't rightly know, but I guarantee you, that's where He does his shopping! All forms of life, humanoid and alienoid, go to the Mall, Melvick . . . I mean, Melvine . . . Ah drat . . ." B.G. never could get his name right. "Mel. And the average visit to the Megaverse Mall, it lasts maybe three or four lifetimes, including the coffee breaks!"

"I don't drink coffee!"

Blind Grapefruit ignored the non sequitur. (P. S. Reader—Byron Preiss Visual Publications will award the first reader who guesses the number of non sequiturs in this book with a

17

complete set of Harry Harrison's *Bill, the Galactic Hero*, signed, in slip-cases and cauterized!) "The first lifetime alone you spend looking for a parking space!"

"No!"

"That's right. And the last lifetime you spend trying to remember where you put your car!"

Melvinge scratched his head at that. "But most people—like me, I think—only have *one* lifetime to begin with!"

"Popular misconception, my boy. We're talking parking lots with accommodation for over 178,000,000 vehicles of every description. And there are generally 336,000,000 vehicles cruising for a space! Anyway, take my word for it, this place makes the Holy Grail look like the Captain Kirk plate in the Star Trek dinnerware collection! It's got just about anything a modern guy of any historical age could want! You got your Elizabethan Codpiece Shoppe with real cods, you got your Edwardian Tuxedo Shoppe with real Edwards—cripes, the list of shops this place has would take an eternity to list. Hey, and they even have a Baseball Card Store with every Topps card you ever lost!"

"Oh dear! Even DINOSAUR ATTACKS?!"

"They got a rare run of Tyrannosaurs eating math teachers the manufacturers decided was far too gross to release!"

Tyrannosaurs eating math teachers! What bliss to contemplate. However, all of this was far too interesting to dwell on the mere ecstasies of nasty instructors waggling bloodily in the mouths of thunder lizards. "Do go on, Blind Grapefruit! I like this much better than the blues."

"Sonny boy, you ain't heard me play the purples yet! You ain't lived till you've heard the Grapefruit blow the purples! But no, you wanna hear about the Meg-Universal Mall. You ever here of pilgrimages to Mecca? Well, the Meg-U-M is absolutely Meccanized! But it ain't easy to go there, no sirree! Lots of visitors never see the Mall. They're distracted by one of the improvised satellite malls. But forget these things . . . they only got one, maybe two thousand emporia! Gypsy malls, they call them. They're erected without permission and when the MUM—that's Meg-Universal Management—finds 'em, they close 'em right up. Still these things get in thirty or forty years' worth of profitable management!"

"You mean some people who say they've seen the Meg-Mall haven't been there at all?!"

"You bet. They just THINK they've seen it. 'See one mall, you've seen The Mall,' some bumper stickers say.

"This place is so great, Melvinge, it's often taken for Christian heaven. You can get blue jeans there and green jeans and chartreuse jeans. There's a cookie shop there that bans walnuts!"

"Good! I hate walnuts!"

"Yes. And a Radio Shack run by Mr. Tesla itself. There's a place where you can get Lithuanian sausage and aardvark-milk cheese! Cripes, and what about the Cinema 100,000 where you can see any movie ever made or that ever *will* be made! We're talking cinematic paradise here, boy!

"Now, for the happy family who's made it to the Mall! Why, these folks will depart Happy Campers with newly acquired lava lamp lights, waterbeds, designer jeans, plastic shoes, rock 'n' roll records—some ecstatic, some sad, some newborn, some dead—but always vowing to come again to the Greatest Mall in Creation!"

At this point Melvinge's eyes were rolling and his tongue was hanging out with awe and salivation! He had a hundred more questions to ask—no, actually a hundred and twenty nine. But the most relevant was the one that popped immediately to his mouth:

"But Blind Grapefruit—have you seen..." He caught sight of Grapefruit's Stevie Wonder Specials and changed verbal tack. "I mean, have you actually *been* to the Meg-Universal Mall?"

A lonely tear tracked down Blind Grapefruit's bearded face. "Why do ya think I sing da blues?"

"Well then!" young Melvinge said, compassionately patting his friend's guitar (named Desi). "Let's go!"

"Yep. One of these days, dat's just what we's gonna do, sonny boy," said Blind Grapefruit. He blew a few chords on his harp, then slurped some of his chocolate-flavored Tang, the drink of Blues astronauts. "Not now, though."

"Not now? But Blind Grapefruit—I *want* to go to the Mall!"

"Of *course* you do, sonny boy. *Everybody* wants to go to da Mall." He strummed a few riffs of his signature tune, "The Hostess Twinkie Blues." "You must train in the ways of truth, righteousness and American Cap Pistolism before you can think of even *approaching* the Mall-to-End-All-Malls!"

"American? What's that?" Melvinge knew what Cap Pistolism was. That was the economic doctrine of Dog Eat Frankfurter, espoused by John Stuart Millionaire. Make that money before that money makes you!

"An arcane spiritual discipline involving Mom, Apple Pie, and Advanced Orthodontics, sonny boy. What I'm tryin' to say is that you gotta work out! Get some muscles . . . grow up . . . gain wisdom. . . . Get a degree in Frisbee Dynamics at the Interstate University. *Then* you can start yapping about making the Quest for the One True Mall!"

Melvinge would have badgered his friend for more nuggets of Truth, but with a few notes of "My Honey Done Left Me for Eddie Haskell," the wise man did a soft shoe directly into the Other.

The Other, of course, being everything that isn't in space or time.

Which, class, we will discuss at a later fate.

Speaking of fates, what, pray tell, has happened to our hero in the Here and Now of our Tale?

Let us change chapters and, *Avaunt!* return to Melvinge's adventures with the Low-rent Parking Lot Gypsies!

Chapter Three

"Teenage Werewolves in Love"
—or—
"When Hairy Met Sally"

> Now Melvinge, on the way to the One True
>   Blue Mall
> He had himself a little trip, he had a little fall.
> He met up with some Gypsies from galaxy of
>   Yonkers.
> They were big, fat, mean, and plenty bonkers!
> > —Blind Grapefruit

Melvinge had always associated "consciousness" with the place where you didn't have dreams, especially bad ones.

Then how come, he asked himself as he woke up smack-dab in the middle of a psychedelic gypsy camp, this looked very much like just about the worst nightmare he'd ever seen?

Off by one of the wagons, a man in paisley pantaloons was playing a German Beach Boys tune ("She had Hun, Hun, Hun, 'til her daddy took her Panzer-tank a-waaaaaay!") on a fiddle while an old gypsy cook stirred matzo bell soup

23

in a kettle abubble over a fire. A particularly fat old woman with waxed mustaches flipped a pack of Parrot Cards spread over a black silk cloth.

Clang clang clang! went the matzo bells in their kettle.

"Polly want a cracker!" went the Parrot Cards.

"Shuddup, you stupid cards!" went the lady gypsy with the mustache (with tiny pink ribbons tied at the ends, Melvinge noticed). "Tell me the future!"

"Awwwkk! Eight stitches! Stitches of eight!"

With enormous disgust the fat woman rose voluminously to her feet and kicked contemptuously at the cards. "Not the *suture,* you idiots! The *future!*" She swung around, her flesh quivering about her like slow-motion lime Jell-O. (Birth weight of these gypsies was about 160 pounds, so you can imagine the proportions we're talking on this babe!) "Snake-spit!" she called.

The hoody gypsy in the leather jacket who had helped clobber Melvinge slithered to attention. "Yeah. Whaddya want?" he said in a bestial Brooklyn accent.

"These Parrot cards . . . dey playing hard to get again. I wants youse to play some Go Fish wid dem—in the East River. Oh, and bring some concrete galoshes along, so's their itty biddy feet won't get wet!"

24

"Oh noo!" screeched the cards. "At the race track tomorrow, the big surprise is High Tail placing first in the fourth race against twenty-to-one odds. At the Aqueduct—"

However, the woman was not listening.

She was staring straight at Melvinge.

"Dat cute little pisher—he's awake!" A greasy grin spread out over her face. She waddled over to the lad and poked him in the chest. "Say, little pisher. You're cute. I got some plans for you!"

Now Melvinge's first inclination was to run away. However, this was very difficult, in fact nigh impossible, since he was heavily manacled with that old gypsy standby, piano wire.

"Struggle all you like, dearie. You'll not get away. Snake-spit put a some serious cub-scout knots in dose bonds." The fat lady smelled of garlic, peanut butter, Lebanon bologna, bagels, and lots more garlic.

"What—what are you going to do with me?"

"First, we ask you some questions, yes?"

"Yeah. Whaddaya think of da Mets dis year?" said Snake-Spit. "Da boys and me, we're real fans!"

"Would you clam it, Snake-Spit! Can't you see I'm talkin' serious business here!" The gypsy turned her moldy cream-cheese-and-lox-bagel face back to her captive pisher. "So then, what's your name, boy?"

"Melvinge."

"Nice name, guy. My name is Magda Nova-leen. I'm the Gypsy Queen hereabouts. So . . . what are you doing in this parking lot, hmmmm?"

"Uhmm . . . well, you see, I was heading for the Megaverse Mall."

"Yeah. So nu? Isn't everybody? What people don't know is, the Elephant Lingerie sale at Bloomy's? It was over last decade. Only good deals dey got at the Mall is on shoes."

Melvinge could not hide his enthusiasm. "Yes! That's why I'm going!"

"Oh! Say, I could sell you some nice Keds right here! Just off the boat from Hong Kong!"

It was easy to turn up his nose at that. Keds! Yuck!

"Yah, yah. You're right, kid. Sorry to insult your sense of taste. So you're going to da Mall, huh? Well, that's okay. We let you go to da Mall, right boys!"

A few grunts sounded from the motley crew of gypsies.

"Yeah . . . but foist, you can do us a lit-tle favor, yeah? We gots a little problem on our hands. We're a self-respectin' bunch of gypsies and proud of our cultural heritage, our family background, and our Green Stamp collection. We got family doing a pizza arcade in da Mall. . . . We were gonna go and do some work for minimum wage but we got lost. . . ."

26

"So *you're* questing for the One True Mall, too."

"Questing?" said Snake-Spit, his voice filled with derision. "Dat sounds like dat Sir Galahad nonsense."

"Yeah!" piped up another mocking gypsy voice. "We're just lookin' for some action!"

"Anyways, what gypsies use to navigate, of course, are *werewolves*!"

"Werewolves? Why werewolves?"

"Werewolves, Melvinge, are humans who turn into wolves at the turn of the Full Moon, right?" said the Gypsy Queen. "But where does the Full Moon go the days it's off? The days of the month when its family, Crescent Moon, Half Moon, and Gibbous Moon, are doing the work?"

"To da Mall, of course!" shouted another gypsy, taking a guzzle of fizzleberry wine, the traditional intergalactic gypsy drink.

"Right on!" said Novaleen. "To the Mall. The principle of "hotter and colder." So it follows that the closer a werewolf gets to the One True Mall, the more wolfy he gets. Come on, Melvinge. Let me introduce you to someone."

She gestured to a couple of big gypsy galoots. They seized the helpless Melvinge's arms and hauled him out past the periphery of the gypsy encampment. There, by a buttress for a highway ramp, a wire pen had been built. In this pen was a profoundly bald creature.

"Melvinge, allow me to introduce you to Larry."

"Hi, Larry."

The miserable creature in the pen just muttered grumpily, sulking like a morose child.

"You have to excuse Larry Halibut," the Gypsy Queen said. "He's from Pittsburgh and he spent most of a stupid senseless life writing space opera and silly-fantasy books for Squiggle Books."

Melvinge cringed. He'd read a few Squiggle Books before and couldn't blame Larry for being depressed.

"Larry is our resident gypsy werewolf."

Melvinge goggled in shock. "But he hasn't got any . . . I mean, I don't even see a tail!"

Larry Halibut muttered and moaned, the sole evidence of wolfhood being a faint howl squeaking through his voice as he said, "So maybe we're *light-years* away from the stupid Mall, already!"

Melvinge's heart skipped a beat. Light-years from the Mall! He'd been assured by that truckstop waitress they were only a few hundred thousand miles away!

"Nope," the Gypsy Queen said. " 'Fraid not, Larry. It's you, chum. You've simply failed yet again. I'm afraid you're not cut out for the noble calling of lycanthropy. I'm afraid that we're going to have to replace you. This is Melvinge, our new candidate."

"You mean you're going to boot me out into the cold universe?" whined Larry.

"No. You can still sit around stirring goulash soup and being grumpy. You can even terrorize the occasional villager, just for old times' sake. But, babycakes, we need a werewolf whose hair *grows*!"

"Look! I got a nice stubble on my chin. Maybe we're closer to the Mall than originally thought."

"Can it, failure."

Novaleen opened the gate and leaned over the prostrate bald werewolf. In Larry's left ear was a glittery jewel earring. Novaleen ripped this off fiercely. Larry Halibut whimpered and scuttled back against the abutment, staring up at his bulky mistress in total fear.

Novaleen affixed the earring (it was the kind that doesn't need piercing, thank goodness—Melvinge didn't have pierced ears. Sometimes Melvinge's parents, Malovia and Ratner, claimed he must have a hole in the *head*—but not in his ears) and stood back to admire it.

"That's the official Gypsy Werewolf Earring, Melvinge. It goes with those blue eyes of yours, don't you think, Snake-Spit?"

"Brown jewels with black eyes? Ugh!"

"Well, *I* like it. So's anyway, folks, why don't you just sit here awhile, eat some nice goulash we'll bring you. And by the by, Larry—show dear Melvinge the Lycanth *ropes*, huh? Teach the pisher. . . ." She started to wobble away, thought of something else to add, and turned around. "And then, when you're through, *bite* him!"

She turned about again and hobbled away.

"*Bite* me?"

"You want I should nip you now?"

"No! I mean—why do you have to bite me? I mean, won't just a friendly *kiss* . . ." He looked at the ugly guy and decided that maybe that would be as bad as a bite. "Or why not just a *handshake*?"

"Nope. Gotta be a bite. That's the way a werewolf passes on the curse. Kinda like cooties, you know?"

"Ugh."

"Yeah, I know what you mean. Me, I got bitten by this little French poodle-wolf back in Pittsburgh halfway through the tenth book of my Stupid World series. Next thing I know, I wake up in somebody *else's* silly-fantasy book series—and a young adult surrealist at that! Sheesh! What a universe, huh? I should have just stayed in bed!"

"Maybe you could just pretend to bite me."

"Look, you think I like this any more than you? I don't like to bite people. But if I don't, Magda Novaleen will dump me in a gigantic bowl of old cold goulash, and listen, bubba, that's plenty awful. So first of all, though, I gotta teach you some werewolf stuff."

"Yeah, and read me *War and Peace* and the *Thousand Nights and a Night*, too."

"Ha ha ha. Hey, that's pretty funny. This silly-fantasy book is really startin' to cook. Gee—you're kinda . . . actually cheering me up!"

Unfortunately, spirits-wise, poor Melvinge was headed just the opposite direction. He did not look forward to becoming a werewolf, let alone working as official gypsy werewolf for Magda Novaleen and company. They probably paid minimum wage and didn't even have company picnics.

"I'm glad somebody's happy," the bound and bothered young man said with a sigh. "I'm kinda getting the blues."

"So anyway, the cardinal rule of werewolfry is—"

But before Larry could get the words out, there was a sudden eruption of the air, followed by a sudden eructation, redolent of hamhocks and black-eyed peas.

"Did somebody say the secret word!"

Standing there, with a great big smile showing great big teeth, his hair bushing out in steel-wool glory, his sunglasses gleaming with pixie dust, was none other than a certain well-beloved purveyor of balladry and world-class moon pies.

"Blind Grapefruit!" said Melvinge. "You've come from the Other to save me!"

"Nope. Don' do rescues an' I don' do windows!" said the musician, grinning and nodding happily. "Me, I do da *blues*!"

"Who's this joker?" said Larry. "You related to that horror-movie blues musician, B.B. Thing?"

"Nope! Actually, I dropped into the story at the wrong *cue* and I'm causing all kinds of problems with the narrative. But I thought, long as I'm here, I could sing da 'Wolfman Blues.'"

"Say," said Larry Halibut. "I'd like to hear *that*!"

"I'd like to get loose of this piano wire!" said our hero, extremely annoyed at his friend.

"Have faith, sonny boy. All will turn out fine. Lemme do my song first, though." Blind Grapefruit cleared his throat and started his song, interspersed with blasts of his harmonica and minor-keyed guitar chords.

My Mama dun told me, she told me loud and
    clear.
Don't go near the woods, boy, look at da woods
    wid fear;
When dat full moon, it riding high and
    stark
It mean the big bad wolf folk are stalking
    in the dark.

(chorus)
I got dose Wolfman Blues

I got da shakes and da howls
I got more fleas than chimpanzees
I got drool runnin' down my jowls.

But me, I was a stupid boy, 'strue, I was
a fool.
I went out and smoked me a cigarette;
thought it was cool.
And the moon, it was big, and the moon it
was high
A great big wolfie thing come and chomp me
on da thigh!

(repeat chorus)
Now I shed on the carpet and scratch myself
to sleep.
When the full moon rises, I howl and I weep.
I gobble foolish people, from meat I can't
abstain;
But my favorite dish is English beef chow
mein.

Larry Halibut seemed absolutely stunned.
"That's it! That's the secret of the werewolves!
Especially the London sort. Nothing we like
better in this world than a nice big bowl of
beef chow mein!"

"See, and you get a nice little song, too. Well,
gotta get along to the point in the story where
I'm actually scheduled to come in," said Blind
Grapefruit. He tipped his hat, bowed, and then,

twinkling, did a backflip into the nothingness of the Other.

"Wow, what a guy," said Larry Halibut. "That sure saves me some breath!" The bald creature got up from his crouching position and opened his mouth, displaying a set of canines that would not have been misplaced on a frothing Tasmanian devil. "Might as well go ahead and bite you and get this over with!"

"Uhmmm . . . uh, hey, Larry. You being a sci-fi and fantasy writer and smart and all, maybe you can explain to me exactly what the Other is, where it fits into the scheme of things, and what the meaning of life is, in the bargain."

"Well, the meaning of life is easy enough. It's in the dictionary under 'L-I-F-E.' But as for that Other business—well, I must admit it's pretty difficult to explain."

"I know that the Other is everything that isn't in Space and Time, and it's where my friend Blind Grapefruit goes. But although he tells me all about the Megaverse Mall *ad infinitum,* he doesn't tell me about what he sees in the Other."

"Yes, it's one of the great Mysteries of Life, along with Stonehenge, the moons of Theta Gamma Three, and where all your socks go in the washing machine." Larry thought for a moment, scratching his bald head. He could have thought as long as he wanted as far as Melvinge was concerned—Melvinge didn't

34

exactly relish the notion of getting chomped by those considerably long, considerably sharp fangs.

Finally Larry Halibut seemed to finish thinking. He held up a finger in a teacherly manner. "Now then, as you know, according to Feinsteinian physics—"

"Wait a minute! You mean *Einstein*. Albert Einstein, finder of the Theory of Relativity."

Larry looked blank. "No. I mean Irving Feinstein, finder of the Theory of Time, Space, and Everything Else. Relativity? What does physics have to do with family matters?"

It was Melvinge's turn to scratch his head, and he would have, except of course for the piano wire.

"Anyway, Feinstein calculated the square root of pi, invented the Prime Rib Numbers, and discovered that Infinity was just the same as zero—only you added a heck of a lot of numbers! He was the guy who discovered that if you weren't in time, and you weren't in space, and you weren't in Eugene, Oregon, then you must be in the . . . Other! Problem was, all known calculations involved time and space! So he had to invent a whole new set of Modular Trigonometry—and this he called the Elvis Equations!"

"The Elvis Equations? You mean as in Elvis Presley?" Melvinge had heard of Elvis, of course. Blind Grapefruit sang some of his songs. He was "dat white boy who learned to sing with grits in his mouth!" "Why Elvis?"

"Feinstein was an Elvis fan, and since Elvis wasn't in Time or Space anymore but thousands swore he wasn't dead—then he must be in the Other."

"Must be a really musical place."

"Exactly. It's where inspiration happens. It's where you go to gather wool. It's bigger than all outdoors and it's smaller than a thimble. Because, Melvinge . . . it's the Plane of Imagination!"

"No kidding. You mean like a B-52 bomber, or a Boeing 747?"

"No, no—I'm talking about a level of quantum mechanics beyond slide rules, beyond computers, beyond infinity, beyond Peoria, Illinois! We're talking the stuff that creates all which is great in living consciousness—like the Sunday funnies, and the works of Shakespeare, and the Mona Lisa, and *Flying Saucer* magazine. We're talking about something so truly wonderful it's priceless, but you can't hold it in your hand and you can't imagine it because it's the *imagining* itself!"

Larry Halibut's eyes got misty and glittery with emotion.

"Wow. You know, and I thought that my Grabovnikon was *cosmic*!"

"Huh?"

"Never mind." Although, come to think of

it, a nice story about the Grabovnikon would stall things some more and maybe Larry would forget all about biting him. "No, wait . . . yeah. I will tell you about the Grabovnikon. It's my time-space machine. It's parked just down the block, and boy is it keen. If I could get out of this wire, we could go and have a look. . . ."

"Nope. Uh uh." Larry shook his head dolefully. "Sorry, pal, but if Magda Novaleen comes back and finds you without teethmarks, I'm in deep goulash."

"No, wait! You didn't finish telling me about the Other. Is it significant that adding an 'M' makes it 'Mother'—kinda like the anti-Other? My mom never liked it when I wool-gathered and—"

But it was too late.

Larry was coming for him, his jaws wide, his teeth sharp. He even managed to spark a feral gleam in his usually torpid eyes.

Chapter Four

Grabovnikon's Rainbow

I got da blues . . . I got da peanut butter and jelly
   roll blues,
My butt's in the gutter and I need me some Meg
   Mall squash shoes.

                    —Blind Grapefruit

Meanwhile, in another time and another
space (although certainly *not* the Other), Harlan the dog worked very, very hard.

Now Harlan was a most remarkable dog.

In fact, he was such a remarkable dog, he
wasn't really a dog at all. Not anymore, anyway. He *used* to be a dog named Fafner—the
resident dog of the Grabovnikon. You could call
him a physical emanation of the Grabovnikon's
personality—the vehicle's alter-ego. Only the
Grab would get bored with the way Fafner
looked, and so Fafner would die and be resurrected under a different alias.

This time he was a dogoid with the remark-
ably beautiful and clever name of Harlan.

And so now (or actually about an hour ago)

Harlan the dogoid was trying to explain to the Grabovnikon what had happened to Melvinge.

"He was captured by *gypsies?*" said the Grab with utter discombobulation, and not a little alarm. "That poor fatherless, motherless boy!"

"He's not an orphan. Malovia is back on their home planet making chicken-feet soup, and Ratner—well, who knows where Ratner is, but he's not dead."

"Well," harrumphed the Grab, its stern voice echoing gruffly throughout the interior of the time-space vehicle. "As far as I'm concerned he's an orphan. I am, for all intents and purposes, his unofficial guardian."

"So what are we going to do?" squeaked the dogoid. "You haven't seen these gypsies. They're plenty fierce. I sure as heck ain't sticking *my* cold nose into their business. I've been discorporated and resurrected twice this year already, and I kind of *like* this identity!"

"Hmm. It does suit you. Well, let me think about this a while, and perhaps with the benefit of my multitude of circuits, logical chips, and RUM[1], we can puzzle out the solution to this dilemma!"

Harlan was not averse to this notion. Melvinge would keep for a while. According to the screen on the control panel, the gypsy tents were tents *and* wagons—the tribe had not slunk

[1]Random Uptight Memory.

into the night. Anyway, this would give Harlan
time to sneak one of Melvinge's sodas out of the
ice box, have himself a chocolate mint doggie
biscuit, and kick up his feet in Melvinge's favorite Lay-Z-Boy recliner, something the grumpy
little snot would *never* have let him do.

So Harlan got himself his snack (along with
one of Melvinge's limited supply of candied
kumquats, just to be ornery), settled down in
front of the back of the screens and controls,
munching and slurping.

Having a break from the disgustingly good
(but a little peculiar) Melvinge was terrific,
Harlan supposed, but the basic problem was
that they needed to get him back. Not because
he and the Grab weren't loyal to the silly little
cuss. They were. But Melvinge was the only one
of them who could operate the complex controls
to drive this thing. If the Grab tried to drive
itself, it tended to short out its neural piggy
banks. And Harlan? Forget it. Harlan was still
on probation for skunk-driving on the Interstate. Anyway, he couldn't drive a stick-shift.

The Grabovnikon, although it had a fancy
name and fancy interior logic circuits and not
one but *two* personalities (three, if you counted
the roving, irascible Harlan), was actually just
a refurbished SuperDuper brand Recreation
Vehicle with a time-space gyroscope in place
of an internal combustion engine. Ratner, a
time/space mechanic of some skill, had fash-

41

ioned the Grabovnikon from spare parts in a Howard Cosmic Junkke Shop, intending to use it in his own quest for the One True Mall.

Unfortunately, one day Ratner went for his usual Monday night of duck pins at the Interstellar Bowl-A-Rama and fell off the face of the neighborhood planetary interstices. Malovia called the police. They even placed an ad in the Interstellar *Space and Times*, to absolutely no avail.

Harlan could well remember the chagrin and heartbreak that Melvinge had experienced at the loss of his father. In fact, although obtaining those squash shoes from the Megaverse Mall was paramount in importance on Melvinge's list, Harlan knew the little guy wouldn't mind running into his old man along the way. In fact, although Melvinge would not admit it, this search for his father could well have been the young man's true, albeit subconscious, reason for undertaking this quest. All this business about a Megaverse Mall was all well and good, Harlan supposed—but a dog knew his boy pretty well. And Melvinge was a good guy whose interest in the ephemeral and mallish things of this existence was healthy and normal, but hardly the primary reason for his existence.

No, thought Harlan, wiping off a tear with the sleeve of his French cuffs as he rose up from the Lay-Z-Boy. *Enough of this nonsense!* He really missed Melvinge and he wouldn't let those darned gypsies keep him for one nanosecond more than absolutely necessary.

Harlan the dogoid (or the caninish humanoid, take your pick) was of the largish Dachshund persuasion, only with longer feet and a shorter tail. He wore a purple frock coat, a frilly French shirt, and half-frame spectacles. He looked every inch a doggish dandy. This appearance he affected in the hope of meeting (and charming, and wooing) female dogoids—his own personal quest on this journey—along with, of course, his eternal pursuit of the One True Fireplug, which naturally had its very own and special corner in the Megaverse Mall.

His one bad habit was chewing licorice gum, a habit never very good for anyone even resembling a dog, since it tended to jam up doggy teeth and jaws. He was by turns sweet and irascible and had been Melvinge's buddy since he was a baby. Although the guy occasionally annoyed Harlan with his naïveté and stupid questions, and Harlan felt the occasional need to strike back with a clever elephant or knock-knock joke to relieve the tension, ultimately—given a little time, a little space—there was no more faithful a dogoid than Harlan.

It was for this reason that Harlan left his snack and treat half-finished and stalked back to Grabovnikon central to see if the computer had come up with a solution.

"So, what's the verdict, Grab?" Harlan barked

impatiently. "How are we going to get Melvinge away from the gypsies?"

A different voice, higher and squeakier than before, answered. It had a definite lisp. "The Grabovnikon is thinking. This is his secondary personality, Williford, speaking. Can I get you some tea and scones? Some jam and biscuits, perhaps?"

Harlan kicked the steel casing of the computer. Lights jiggled and winked with alarm. "Time is up in there, Grab. Take the thinking cap off and tell me what you've come up with!"

"Really, Mister Harlan! You needn't resort to violence. I shall seek out Master Grabovnikon in the recesses of his sanctum sanctorum and notify him that you wish to speak with him."

"No time for that, either!" Harlan kicked the casing again. Framed pictures on the side of the time/space vehicle rattled, and cutlery clattered to the floor. "C'mon Grab. Get your brain percolating!"

A voice elbowed the lispy persona and let its presence be known with pure baritone.

"That was a short break, Harlan!"

"So I'm worried about the kid! So sue me! What have you come up with?"

"After considerable thought I have come up with the most intelligent and feasible solution for this problem before us!"

"So spit it out, already! We haven't got all millennium!"

The lights on the computer banks glittered with enthusiasm.

"Simple. These pesky gypsies? We nuke 'em!"

Chapter Five

"A Short Clip About the Ears"
—or—
"Return of the Wolfy-Man"

I been to Kansas City, Jupiter;
   I been to Alpha Centauri;
Of all the tales that I dun heard
   Dis is the bagelest story.
                —Blind Grapefruit

WITNESS *this scene of primal conflict!*

SEE *the supernatural creature*—a man who barks at the moon!—*bare his sharp fangs!*

VIEW *the poor victim, tied up in piano wire, tremble with fear, knowing full well that the werebeast could forget to just take a little nip of the thigh and instead go for his naked jugular!*

SMELL *the sweat!*

WATCH *the pathetic werewolf try to grow hair on his pale bare body!*

"Grrrrrrrrrr!" said Larry Halibut, the gypsy werewolf.

"Oh dear!" said Melvinge, the helpless victim.

He wished that he had taken that extra class in lip-throws in the marital martial arts series at the Y.

The werewolf, crouching low to the ground, stalked his prey, snapping his jaws fiercely together. Larry the Werewolf actually looked rather pathetic without hair—but those fangs were the real thing, no question.

Melvinge closed his eyes and prepared for chomping.

Nothing, however, happened.

Almost too afraid to look, Melvinge took a peep. Sitting before him was Larry the Werewolf, scratching himself, looking dejected and forlorn.

"I can't do this," Larry said.

"You can't?" said Melvinge hopefully.

"Well, not the way that batty witch Magda Novaleen wants it done, anyway. Not with blood and pain and all that disgusting stuff. Maybe that's been my main problem. I'm just not into all that melodrama and violence. Novaleen wanted me to go to the gypsy psychoanalyst, Dr. Sigmund Doofus, but the guy says since I'm a carnivore he couldn't handle me. He doesn't do Foodian therapy."

"So what . . . I mean . . . maybe we could both escape? We could be pals."

"Sorry, I'm too much of a cur for that. Nope, gotta at least turn you into a werewolf. So . . ."

And with a quick lunge the werewolf named Larry darted around Melvinge and nipped him lightly upon the left buttock.

It was rather like a booster shot. One little snippet of pain and that was all.

"Ouch," said Melvinge. Then: "That's it?"

"That's all it really takes. If the werewolves of history had been a little less nuts, *everybody* would have become werewolves, and life today would be a lot simpler for we bestial folk."

"This is going to make me into a werewolf?"

"Don't you feel the follicles foliating?"

"No."

"Hmmmm. Maybe we aren't that close to the Megaverse Mall after all. Maybe—"

But then, suddenly, Melvinge began to itch.

We're talking major I'm-going-nuts-with-this-sensation *itching*, all over his body—especially his face.

He was growing hair at a most alarming rate!

And the heck of it was, he was tied up.

Melvinge couldn't *scratch*.

"Yee—OWWWWWWWWWWWWWL," he cried, and he could not believe his own ears. His cry turned in mid-vowel from a quite human wail of annoyance to a most wolfy baying-at-the-moon kind of howl.

Melvinge was turning into a werewolf!

The wretched yowl attracted the attention of the gypsies. Magda Novaleen and company hurried down the alley formed by the gypsy caravans, huffing and puffing with excitement and exertion like a bunch of kids who've just heard the tinkle of an Intergalactic Ice Cream Truck's bell.

"So what have we got here!" said Novaleen, her eyes glittering like garnets.

"Ya see, Novaleen," Snake-Spit said, "we're closer to the Mall than you thought!"

For Melvinge's part, he was too busy itching to worry about how close or how far the Megaverse Mall was. The horrendous itching was driving him so crazy he was simply going absolutely buggy with frustration because, of course, the piano wire prevented him from scratching.

He fell to the ground and rolled around, howling and wailing with awful discomfort.

"Good job, Larry!" said Novaleen.

Larry grunted and sulked disconsolately back into his corner, licking his chops and glaring at all that hair with envy.

"Shall I take off the piano wire?" asked Snake-Spit.

"Yes!" howled Melvinge. *"Yessssssssss!"*

"Maybe." Novaleen prodded the captive neo-werewolf with a fat toe poking through her lizard-leather sneakers. "But only if the guy promises no funny business."

"I promise!" cried Melvinge, flopping around. "I promise!"

"Get out one of Larry's spare leashes, just in case!" ordered Magda Novaleen. "Right! Now, take off da piano wire and let's see just what kind of werewolf we've got on our hands."

"A very itchy one, from the look of things," muttered Larry.

"Stay still or I ain't gonna be able to do it!" Snake-Spit warned the flopping Melvinge.

Melvinge stayed as still as he could, fidgeting despite himself, as the gypsy unwound his bonds. Melvinge then hopped up and began to scratch himself furiously. He realized with some chagrin that he was scratching himself with his foot!

"Here you go, Mel," said Novaleen. "This should help!" She gestured and one of the gypsies tossed a bucket of cold water on Melvinge.

Actually, it did help. Only it was also excruciatingly chilly.

"Thanks," said Melvinge, his teeth chattering.

"Don't mention it, babycakes," said Novaleen. "So then, welcome to the clan!" Her gypsy henchman snapped on the leash.

"Hey! I did promise!"

"Let's just call it insurance," said Snake-Spit.

"Let's just call it normal procedure," grumbled Larry Halibut, who was promptly rewarded with a kick in the ribs for his trouble.

"So like we said, welcome!" said Novaleen. "You are now the tribe's official werewolf. You get a half a kopek a year and we only charge half a kopek a year for your room. Oh, and you get all the goulash you can eat."

"And all the kicks in the ribs you want," murmured Larry, showing canines at Snake-Spit.

"Actually, what I really want," said Melvinge, "is to get out of here and go to the Mall."

"Oh, you get to go to the Mall!" promised Novaleen. "You even get to sit guard duty at cousin Bela's Lugosi stand and eat all the goulash bagels you want. Only you gotta stay here with us and do that!"

Melvinge started jumping up and down.

"Harlan! The Grabovnikon!"

"We're very sorry," sneered Snake-Spit. "You're just going to have to forget about your friends."

"That would be very hard to do," said Melvinge cheerfully, "since they certainly haven't forgotten about me." He pointed past the gypsies' bulky shoulders. "You see, here they come, rolling over one of your caravans! And Harlan can't even drive a stick-shift!"

Stunned and aghast, Magda Novaleen turned, only to be rewarded with the ghastly sight and sound of a gigantic recreational vehicle rolling over one of the gypsy wagons, crushing it flat as a potato pancake.

Ker——*RUNCH!*

52

"My Parrot Cards!" cried Magda Novaleen.
Sqaa——*WAWWWWWWK!*

Feathers and cards fluttered outward from the crushed van. Outraged cards flapped away.

"You'd have thought they'd have seen that coming," commented Larry, his moroseness momentarily lifted by this welcomed sight of devastation and decimation.

The Grabovnikon halted just yards away. A door opened and Harlan the dogoid leaped out, clutching a Thompson submachine gun to his chest, a cigar poking from exposed molars. The gun coughed. Pre-chewed bubblegum bullets streaked out from the muzzles, supplying their own speed lines with trailing gum strands and spittle.

They wrapped around the gypsies like melted plastic, getting in their eyes and hair and generally gumming up their entire operational ability, big time.

Onward the Grabovnikon plunged—straight toward the newly hirsute Melvinge!

"No! Wait!" Melvinge yelped. "Harlan! You forgot the parking brake!"

"Well, gosh—I can't remember everything!"

Still, Harlan dropped the Thompson and hopped back into the runaway time/space vehicle.

The thing charged on nonetheless. Melvinge turned around. Running for cover was probably useless, but it was better than getting run over and squished together in gypsy juice.

However, with a horrendous *SCREEEEE-EECH!* of brakes, the Grabovnikon stopped.

Not before giving the gypsies a good swift kick with its bumpers, sending them earrings-over-derrières into the werewolf watering trough. But it stopped all the same.

"Harlan! You did it! I love you!"

"Please," said Harlan, peering through the bug-splattered windshield, his cigar bobbing and dropping ashes onto the dashboard as he hit the comm switch. "Just a simple scratch behind the ears will do! Cripes, Melvinge. You look like you got sprinkled with Crabgrass Lawn-Gro!"

"Explanations later!" cried Melvinge, turning a frightened gaze back to the gypsies. Sure enough they were still conscious, scrambling out of the werewolfy mess.

And plenty ticked off, from the looks of them.

He ran up to the door of the Grabovnikon, hopped on board and skittered hairily to the controls.

"Welcome back, sir!" intoned the rounded vowels of the Grab's voice.

Harlan obligingly relinquished the controls.

"We gotta get out of here! That Magda Novaleen's a witch! She might turn the Evil Smell on us!"

"Don't you mean the 'Evil Eye,' sir?" said the Grab.

"You haven't got an up-close whiff of the garlic on those guys!" Melvinge swiftly shifted into reverse, backed the Grabovnikon into another gypsy caravan (smashing it thoroughly), yanked the thing into first, revved the time/space engine and gunned it into a fifteen-minute time/space skip that put them squarely back on the Interstate, toward the Mall.

They could not have seen it, but behind them, Magda Novaleen the Gypsy Queen raised a fist and a curse.

"I'll get you for this, Melvinge!" she promised. "And by the end of this book, too!"

Chapter Six

Melvinge, the Fork in the Road, and Other Utensils Along the Way (Including Truck Stop Greasy Spoon)

I got da travelling Blues—I been up and down da
  dirty road.
My mama don't love me no more and I feel like
  a toad.
But whenever my life's a mess and my heart's in
  a fix.
I just haul my wheels out onto Root Sixty-Six!
                                    —Blind Grapefruit

Class!

Attention please. I don't want to see those
eyes sneaking past this page and over to the
television set. Books are *good* for you. Books
are educational.

What? You get enough education in your
school? Well I don't see any PhD's hanging on
your wall. Oops, excuse me, Drs. Frankenstein
and Jekyll. I guess there's always an exception
to the rule.

To start this chapter, as the Grabovnikon
grunts and growls its way down the road

bearing its wolfy and doggy cargo (woof woof!) perhaps it would be best to pause, catch our breaths, drink some Avocado soda, have a poppyseed bagel and talk about the Interstate itself.

The Interstate is a sort of current or wrinkle or warp or effluence of matter, energy, insubstantial thoughtforms, and tourists which runs through Time, Space—and of course through the Other.

Although it is called a road, and it has all the accoutrements of highways—ramps, lit signs, mileage markers, traffic signs, dead skunks— it is in fact something quite a bit more than your normal Earth-type road, as you might have guessed by the gist so far of this story.

Allow me to quote from that eminent scholar, scientist, and specialist on this very subject, Ducktor Daniel Manus Pinkwater, as he discourses on this very subject in his excellent *New York Times* non-fiction bestseller, *Pinkwater's Universe or How I Learned to Love Black Holes, Singularities, and Boiled Tripe and Leek Stew*:

"In practical terms," Ducktor Pinkwater writes,

a number of elements must converge in order to move freely along the Interstate. Some individuals posses the ability to simply embark at will. Often a highly com-

58

plex series of circumstances must obtain. [Translation: It's a weird thing, this Interstate.]

Ducktor Pinkwater goes on:

One might be walking along, [on the Interstate] going about one's business, having enjoyed a Turkish specialty lunch at Eat-A-Rama [sic] in Poughkeepsie, N.Y. One might be running a slight fever, say 99.1, the result of a mild rhinovirus [sick]. On this particular occasion, the subject may have had a particularly potent helping of the house onion sauce. The sun might be low in the sky, it being about the time of the Autumnal Equinox, and the random mix of industrial pollutant suspended over Poughkeepsie might act as a filter, giving an orange cast to the light. The confluence of these elements, relatively insignificant in themselves, might combine with a fleeting moment of mental distraction, an astronomical alignment, an errant microwave from Mr. Levent Ozgur's state-of-the-art gyro apparatus, and cause one of those spontaneous disappearances which are hushed up by the authorities. We know that the abruptly departed has simply stepped onto the Interstate. Disconcerting, at first, for the individual who arrives sucking his toothpick without a thought in his head. But Time, Space, and the Other being more or less infinite, he has plenty of time to get used to the idea. [Translation: It's a weird place, this Interstate.]

But please be patient; Ducktor Pinkwater takes another stab in his next two paragraphs:

More complex is the case of an individual who appears to become nonexistent for a mere fraction of a second and, in that time, arrives on the Interstate and stays there, while almost simultaneously resuming his activities in the reality we're usually caught up in.

Of course, all this suggests an explainable, technologically oriented approach to the Interstate—which may well be a wrong one. The principles involved might have nothing to do with anything we'd expect! [Translation: This is a *really* weird place, this Interstate!]

However, it is best that we continue with this narrative, since just how *weird* the Interstate truly is will become more than apparent during the course of the story.

* * *

"I'm hungry!" announced Harlan the next day (give or take the few fifteen-minute time-space skips utilized by the Grabovnikon in escaping the gypsies). He pointed a recently painted nail past the windshield. (Harlan was into makeup and body paint and stuff) toward a roadside stand marked PINKIE'S: WORLD CLASS DOGS. "And I really crave a chili dog with lots of onions, relish, and Uncle Edgar's Famous Tripe Sauce. Whaddya say, Melvinge?"

Melvinge shook his hairy head and sighed. "I'd really rather keep going. We've got to find that Mall. Besides, I might catch fleas at that place!"

Melvinge, in truth, was having difficulty adjusting to the fact that he was now a werewolf.

Last night he'd done a quick access of the Grab's memory on the subject of werewolf cures. Actually, the Grabovnikon's computer didn't have a clue—but it did figure that since everything else was at the Megaverse Mall, then surely so must be a cure for Lycanthropic Oopsiosis, the official term for accidental werewolfry.

Verdict: Get thee hence to the Mall, just as fast as thy little hairy buttest cannest.

The conundrum of this situation was that the closer Melvinge got to the One True Mall, of course, the less "were" he became and the more "wolf." In other words, the "nearer," the "furrier." Nonetheless, it was something that had to be done and done as quickly as possible—if only to get himself a gross of Hartz Mountain Flea and Tick Collars.

For this reason, Melvinge would have much preferred to stay on the Grabovnikon and enjoy a spam and banana sandwich rather than stop at some ugly greasy spoon in the middle of the ternpike (a turnpike with a lot of birds) for a stupid chili dog.

However, Harlan *had* saved him from a life of cold goulash and imprisonment in a gypsy pen with a weird guy named Larry, so this had to be a contributing factor in his decision.

"Oh, Harlan. Do you *really have* to have a chili dog?"

"Oh yes, puh-*leeeeeeeze?*" Harlan got down on his knees and begged, a momentary relapse into his doggie background. Normally Harlan was alternately proud, argumentative, irascible, and just plain contentious—a regular canine tornado with a vocabulary. However, when it came to chili dogs, the creature simply melted into a pathetic puddle of helpless hunger.

"Okay."

"Oh, please! I shall shine your shoes, Melvinge! I shall read to you from the works of Balzac! I shall do the dance of the Seven Jerry Vales for your entertainment! I shall—" The dog blinked. "Did you say 'okay'?"

"That's what I said!" Melvinge pushed the button that took the Grabovnikon off automatic. He downshifted, wheeled the vehicle onto a ramp, and parked in the lot, running over numerous candy bar wrappers and empty beer cans in the process. "Here we go, Harlan. You need some money, pal?"

The astonished Harlan turned his gaze toward the sight of the roadside stand, the neon signs twinkling in his eyes. 'Pinkie's' proclaimed a frozen fireworks display. Holographic cherubs and devils danced the Watusi along the electric-blue top of the cheap stucco building. Even in here, Melvinge fancied he could smell the odor of deep fried turtle's tongue, the favorite Interstate roadside-stand taste treat.

"No," said Harlan. "No, I've got some money saved up in my bedroom! And I'd better get dressed, too! After all, there is a dress code at Pinkie's."

"Just don't forget your bib. You remember what happened the last time you ate chili dogs. We had to spend a fortune in dry-cleaning bills!"

Actually, the only dress code at Pinkie's was the next lower on the rung below "casual dress"—namely, "casualty dress." However, Harlan liked to dress up at the drop of a top hat, and for the dogoid, the opportunity of eating a chili dog was certainly sufficient occasion.

Melvinge whiled away the time reading an

article about snarking out on the Interstate in an issue of *Boy-Thing's Life*. Yesterday had been too much excitement for the Grab—it was in an uncommunicative mode, doubtless picking belly-button lint from its metaphorical belly-button.

"Ready!" announced Harlan, jumping out from his private quarters, newly regarbed. He twirled about to show Melvinge the full splendor of his outfit. Harlan wore a black tie, a tux, and a cummerbund. Upon his feet were spit-shined shoes glowing almost as much as the neon of Pinkie's sign. "So, Melvinge. What do you think? Pretty sharp, huh?"

"Donald Trumpoid, eat your heart out!" said Melvinge, applauding his companion.

Harlan took a deep bow. "Thank you. Thank you. Now, shall we venture forthwith outward to dine upon yon chili dogs?"

"Let me make sure I've got a couple bottles of Pepto-Abysmal in my back pocket first."

"Just jeans, huh?" Harlan sniffed haughtily.

"Yeah. I'm just going to have a shake and some fries. Nothing formal for me!"

Harlan nodded. "Very well, but you realize of course that with your choice of comestibles we shall have to dine in separate portions of this eating establishment."

"Actually, Harlan, I was rather counting on that."

The interior of Pinkie's was packed with people, interstellar travellers and Interstate creatures of incredible variety, all clamoring for their fair portions of this popular motorway food.

"I'll have a dinkum burger and a side order of French-fried popsicles!" cried a bellicose bilko-beast from Betelgeuse.

A fake-aardvark beast from false-Pluto waved a pseudo-pod. "A kumquat milkshake, please!"

Kumquat milkshakes!

Now Melvinge was getting excited.

The dining area itself was hardly the formal sort that Harlan's outfit would imply. In fact, it was a total shambles. Upon the walls were various signatures, mugshots and footprints of the sundry Interstate souls brave enough to actually eat here.

Actually, to be fair, Melvinge had to admit to himself that he'd seen worse. Also, once you got used to the noise and the crush and the sound of Martian krap music ("rap with a capital K for kick, girls and boys") and the smell of burnt tortoise tails (Melvinge preferred his tortoise tails medium rare) it really wasn't too bad—and it was a fairly typical watering spot for an Interstate comfort station (although those Johnny-on-the-Spots in the back hardly passed muster).

Yes, you had your typical motley group of folks here.

There was Winston Churchill, for example, having a cup of tea and a honey-dipped donut. And there was Alexander the Great, standing on a stool to get his mitts on a straw for his shish kebab soda.

"Look, Melvinge," said Harlan. "A triceratops on training wheels by the drive-thru. I thought triceratops were outlawed on the ternpike after the great Pterodactyl Runway disaster."

Melvinge nodded. "That was *until* the Bureau for the Advancement of Mesozoic Creatures pointed out that that was highway mismanagement and poor planning. So now any land reptile can go on the Interstate as long as it's got wheels. These smaller places usually didn't let the big ones in, but the medium ones usually fit under the drive-in roofs. Still, they gotta watch out for the carnivores."

"Why? They carry out the customers too?"

"No, you've got to pass an IQ test to get a driver's license for the Interstate."

"Oh. Right."

"No." Melvinge nudged his friend and winked. "They eat *all* the chili dogs! Every one!"

Harlan's eyebrows shot up. "Ban the beasts!"

It took a little while to get up to the counter, but Melvinge and Harlan spent it fruitfully discussing analytic philosophy with Martin Heidegger and Bertrand Russell and then cosmic puppetry with Jim Hensen and Kermit the Frog.

However, they did finally make it to the front of the line, and Melvinge was able to place his order.

"I'll have a kumquat shake please. And my friend Harlan here will have a chili dog."

The owner, a grumpy amorphoid fleshopod named Sid, stared down at the duo with suspicion. "What kinda truck you got out there, chums?"

"Truck?" said Melvinge, a little peeved. "That's no truck. That's the Grabovnikon."

"That's one of them fancy new SOT machines!" cried an anonymous Andromedan, amiably.

"SOT machines? Looks like a SNOT machine to me!"

Sid was in a very bad mood. He didn't care for dogoids and his wife was a werewolf and a particularly nagging one, so he took every chance to snub the species.

"Look guy, don't insult my wheels!" said Melvinge, particularly sensitive to this line of attack since the RV was a particularly lame-looking one, what with all the additions his father had put on it. "Yeah, and, like, you've got the classiest joint on the highway, huh? Why'd they let you set up, to draw all the flies away from the others?"

Incensed, Sid's big bulging eyes bugged further. His amorphoid frame amorphoided even fleshopoddier.

"Would you gentlemen cease and desist!" Harlan moaned. "I really and truly *would* like my chili dog. And I suspect that a nice cold kumquat shake will not only cool my companion down significantly, it will send us on our way and it will get our vehicle out of your parking lot."

Sid grunted and grinned. That seemed okay with him.

"Kumquat shake!" he screamed to a small man working amongst the machines in the galley feverishly. "And a chili dog? Whatcha want? Small, medium, or Absolutely Mammoth?"

"Oh, Absolutely Mammoth, *please*!" Harlan's eyeballs rolled joyfully in their sockets.

"That man in the back there. The chief cook and bottle washer," said Melvinge, trying to peer past the steam of the chili dog smog. "Do you think he looks familiar?"

Harlan, a full head shorter than Melvinge, had to stand on his tippy toes and crane even further, which was particularly difficult since they'd neglected to bring a crane along. "Hmmm. I see what you mean. Still I can't quite place the face. Don't suppose all that steam and ketchup on it helps much." Harlan bounced back down onto the balls of his feet. "Still, you must realize that we'll be seeing lots and lots of beings, human and otherwise, on this trip. After a few hundred million, faces start repeating. Why, did you realize, Melvinge, that the occupants of the planet Squeegee, quite far out of the Milky Way galaxy, indeed all the way into the Snickers galaxy, all look like Pee Wee Herman and derive their names from the Tenafly White Pages?"

Melvinge *wasn't* aware of that, nor did he particularly care. He was beginning to get annoyed with the fact that, despite the universe being so vast and incomprehensible, much of it had to do with the state of New Jersey. It made the pain of never having visited that remarkable mythical state all the more poignant.

Still, that was another Quest, wasn't it?

Maybe, after the Megaverse Mall, they could do New Jersey on their way to Harlan's personal dreamquest—the Quest for the Holy Hamburg Grill, that Sacred Place in the Royal Province of Queens.

"Well?" Harlan prompted.

"You're right."

Harlan put a comforting paw-oid on his friend's shoulder. "You thought he looked like Ratner, didn't you?"

"Yes. I guess I did think he looked like my father."

"Unlikely. Besides, I know for a fact Ratner is allergic to pickles. This establishment must be positively *bursting* with dills and koshers and gherkins and oh, every type of pickle that

69

exists! To say nothing of the relish!"

"Relish?" said Sid, hoisting their order toward them. "You say you want some relish?"

"Yes, please!"

Sid grabbed a hand-pod full of sweet relish, dotted with onion and red pepper, and slapped it onto the colossal slab of juicy, chili-ed, dog-in-a-bun that was Harlan's order.

Then he put another hand-pod full of the stuff in Melvinge's kumquat shake!

Melvinge's jaw dropped. "Gee, thanks! Does that cost extra?"

"Naw. Not here at Pinkie's. Ain't you seen our ad? Condiments on the House!"

Oh, thought Melvinge as he accepted his delightfully purple and green frosty treat. So *that* was what all that stuff was, dripping down off the roof.

"Thank you, kind sir," said Harlan, accepting his chili dog. They then paid their money and decided that perhaps they should take their stuff back to the Grabovnikon rather than consume it at these—let's face it—rather cheesy and uninviting tables here.

Besides, Plato and Socrates were drinking Hemlock Surprises at one, and boy, was Melvinge sick of talking about philosophy.

As Melvinge and Harlan left, a diminutive member of the kitchen staff wiped the chili sauce from his face and trundled over to the window, scratching his head. He coughed.

"Hey pal!" said Sid. "This ain't your coughing break! Save the germs for the Bacteria-Cheese Burgers!"

The kitchen help looked totally baffled. He looked as though the sight of Grabovnikon was bringing back distant but vital memories.

"I ain't seen you look so spaced, guy, since I found you tracking whipped cream in from being lost on the Goober Dessert!"

The kitchen help mouthed an attempt at a word. "Rat . . . Rat . . . Rat . . ." He looked at Sid. "Rat fink!"

Sid kicked him. "Don't call me names. Now get back to work. We're almost out of French flies out here!"

The man shook his head and trooped back to the Lice Box.

Chapter Seven

Sdark Happenings

Now little boy, I know you broke, I know you blue
I know you bills dey scream, your creditors dey
   bark.
But honey child, my blues buddy, I tellin' you.
Stay away from that awful blob, Sdark the
   Loan Shark.

                    —Blind Grapefruit

    No sooner had Melvinge closed the door to the Grabovnikon, so that he and Harlan could enjoy their treats in peace, no sooner had Sid the amorphoid fleshopod given one last sneer of distaste at the glorified RV in his parking lot, than did the backyard of his establishment begin to undulate with some urgency.

    For, you see, the backyard—fronting the Goober Dessert—was actually no backyard at all, but rather the monstrous form of Sdark, the Loan Shark, come to collect a past-due payment from Sid and Pinkie's.

    "Sid," called an obnoxious gurgle like the sound of thunder gargling. "Sid, the amorphoid fleshopod! It is I, Sdark, the Loan Shark. Where's my dough?"

Sdark, the Loan shark!

Sid's uppermost heart filled his throat as he peered through the hot dog smog, up toward the mammoth form bulking before him like a double pancake stuffed with apple sauce, plus bloodshot eyes and enormous gnashing teeth. Finny hands held a notebook. On the front of his gray body were the outlines of a metal bank vault, complete with lock.

Sdark the Loan Shark's very own cyborg bank. The creature was a cy-bank!

"Good gopher gravy!" Sid whimpered. A shiver amorphoided his fleshopodic body gelatinously.

"How's business?" Sdark said in a terrifying whisper. Sid thought he could see Captain Ahab, Robert Shaw, and the Mormon Tubercular Choir stuck between those sharp, enormous teeth.

Sid flopped down to his knees. "Oh please don't kill me!" he wailed.

The customers were so petrified by this scene that they let their chili dogs go cold.

Those terrible bloodshot sharkoid eyes widened. "Am I to understand that you haven't got 12,650 zlotys for me?" asked the loan shark. He was motionless except for the regular undulations of his gill slits, and a slight clicking sound from the lock on the bank vault in his huge body.

74

"Come out here, Sid, so we don't have to shout at each other, eh?"

"I really don't—"

"I said get your sorry pod out here, Sid!"

Sid obliged, not getting off his knees, just wallowing out in abject, jellyfish terror. Now Sid was rather the size of a giant walrus, and no attendee of Weight Watchers. However, Sdark was at least four times the size of a Greyhound bus. The loan shark dwarfed the fast food shop's proprietor.

"I've got six thousand!" said Sid. "Somebody has been gleeping the customers!"

"I'm sorry to hear that, really I am. You want to get ready now?" The jaws began to work and a spray of saliva shot off into the dust right by Sid's feet. Sid cringed. Sdark smelled like a hot day at the wrong side of the pier.

"Please don't do it," Sid begged. "Take the six thousand. Let me live."

"I will take the six thousand," Sdark said. "But as to letting you live—well, Sid, I like you, really I do—and I'd like to let you live, but consider what that would do to my reputation." Sdark inserted a cigarette. Lit it. Coughed. Smoke poured out of him and it took a full minute for him to recover, by which time the whole area was covered with a pall. "I'm trying to build a reputation."

"Oh Sdark, you've got a beautiful reputation,"

the fleshopod blubbered. "Everybody hates and fears you."

"It's nice of you to say that," the shark whispered like the Godfather with a head cold. "But you see, that's the whole point. If I should fail to cause you to die in horrible agony, word might get around. People talk, Sid, they really do. What would happen to my business if I didn't make an example of you? It isn't my actual cruelty and viciousness that matters—it's the perception of my cruelty and viciousness. People would say that I let you off and pretty soon . . . well, there's no point going on like this, really there isn't. But I tell you what—and don't let this get around—I'm going to kill you really fast. You won't feel a thing. Now don't say that Sdark never did anything for you. Ready?"

Sid fell onto the ground, wiggling about like a worm trying to escape a descending hook. "Wait!" he cried.

"Wait?" The gigantic shark's teeth wobbled, they stopped so quickly. Nonetheless, something—perhaps the odor of kumquat shakes on Sid's apron—stopped the shark in midbite.

Sid gestured toward Pinkie's. "I'll give you the stand."

"I get that anyway. I'll sell it to another schmuck like you!" Sdark wheezed with laughter at the very thought. The smell of rotten sardines wafted from his open jaws.

Sid cast about desperately for some other

plan, some other angle. And then he remembered those two annoying little geeks and their silly-looking Winnelumbago they claimed was a—ha!—time/space machine. He turned and checked. Yeah, those goofs were still choking on the chili dog and shake. The RV was still in the parking lot!

A smile quivered onto his fat doughy features. "How about a time/space machine? A good time/space machine is worth forty, fifty thousand. I'll give you a time/space machine for the difference."

"Let's see it."

"There! It's there!"

The loan shark swung its neckless face. Observed. Beady eyes went back to the roadside-stand owner. "That thing? That looks like a Winnelumbago that some nut with a loose screw tacked a few SOTty coils onto! That's not worth much at all."

"I think you're wrong." Sid got up and began bargaining with all his powers of persuasion. "Look at those lines. What we've got here, my friend, is a most definite *classic*. Look at those lines! Look at that hood ornament! I mean, the hood ornament alone is priceless!"

"It hasn't got any lines.... And I've seen better hood ornaments on 1967 Volkswagen buses!"

"I swear, you go down to Tarzana World, Big

Al Morhaim will give you thirty thousand for it! At least!"

The loan shark sucked his tooth in contemplation. "Okay. Maybe I can allow you six thousand—that will leave you six hundred and fifty shy."

"What will you do to me for that?" asked Sid, relieved but still a little suspicious.

"Let's see . . . for anything over five hundred, you have to die. But I like you, Sid, I really do—so here's what I'll do. I'll take the SOT machine. . . ."

"It's called the Grabovnikon."

"Like I said, I'll take the Grabovnikon, and the six thousand, and you can owe me the rest at triple interest, payable next time . . . and I'll bite your head off, for a treat. Deal?"

"Deal!" said the fleshopod.

"Okay. Head first!" And with a lightning-sharp lunge, the shark chewed off the topmost portion of Sid.

Then, chomping slowly, savoring its morsel, it turned to its new toy.

Since it figured the best way to carry the Grabovnikon was in its stomach, the shark simply gobbled the thing whole and swallowed it down.

Then it turned and wallowed back into the sand of the dessert, headed for a place where (it was pretty sure) it could get a good deal for the Grabovnikon.

Meantime, the body of Sid, still standing, sprouted another head on its side, blinked, smiled, and laughed. "That idiot! That was just a pod it bit off!"

The kitchen helper suddenly ran past him after the loan shark.

"Hey!" Sid shouted. "Guy! Where the heck you think you're going? We've got to fry up those French flies. Get the wildebeest lard out of the storage!"

"Sorry, Sid," said the man. "The shock of seeing the Grabovnikon swallowed jogged my memory out of the amnesia it was suffering. My name is really Ratner! I created that thing! And that loan shark just swallowed my son, Melvinge!"

With astonishing speed, Sid's kitchen help disappeared into the Goober Dessert.

Sid just shook his head. "That's the third amnesiac this month! What do they think Pinkie's is, a memory bank?" He turned around to find his customers and kitchen crew regarding his new head poking from his side with awe. "Hey! What are you jokers staring at! Ain't you ever seen a good businessman get ahead?"

The customers groaned and went back to their food.

Chapter Eight

Call Me Ishmael, But Don't Call Me Late for Dinner

I got da blues, I got da loan shark blues.
I'm stuck here in his stomach with these old
    wornout shoes.

                —Blind Grapefruit

When Melvinge left for his Quest, he knew that so far in his life he'd missed adventures. But he had no idea that on this journey he'd experience such *mis*adventures!

Both Melvinge and Harlan hardly took notice when there was a slight quiver, a slight quake in the Grabovnikon. Certainly the Grab took no notice, or the thing would have pronounced its misgivings in its rich, deep voice reminiscent of the bass singer for the Temptations. After all, they had experienced plenty of Interstate quakes, or highway hops, before. Existing as a path through Space, Time, and the Other had its physical pressures, and these pressures often registered on the Richter Scale, (as well as the Hot One Hundred of some planets' popular teen radio stations).

However, both Melvinge and Harlan certainly knew something was wrong when the dregs of Melvinge's kumquat shake splooshed into Melvinge's face, and the last squishy morsel of chili dog splatted onto the dogoid's lap.

Something is wrong, thought Melvinge, spluttering purple glop with surprise. *Something is very wrong.*

The Grabovnikon immediately twirled roof-over-axles as though to underscore the significance of this wrongness.

"Oh dear," said the Grab, a high hiccup in its usually confident voice. "Hang onto your haaaaaaaaaaats!"

A skip, a flip. A flop, a bop. The vehicle bumped and thumped like a toaster on a rollercoaster. It scuppered and uppered and then thuppered through what seemed like a thundering water-slide ride and then, with the booming resonant echo of a weight splashing into a pool of hot saltwater taffy at the bottom of a mine shaft, it slopped to a quivering, shaking, absolutely feverish halt.

"Goodness!" said Harlan. The entire front of his clothing was splattered red and hot pink with the chili sauce. The last bite of the dog part of the chili dog was wedged ridiculously in one ear, like some absurd frankfurter headphone. "What happened? Were we struck by some runaway truck?"

"Grab?" Melvinge said, shakily getting back to his feet. The screens were out; the instrument bank held no readings.

"It would appear," intoned the Grabovnikon, sounding like a bad telephone connection, "from all indications, that we have been swallowed by a loan shark!"

Swallowed by a loan shark!

What a concept! What a spectacle!

Melvinge was absolutely thunderstruck by the very notion. It was as though he had just been told that he had a surprise birthday gift from the planet Neptune. (Only of course, all in all, he'd rather have something cold and old from Neptune than be sitting in the midst of some monstrous loan shark's digestive system.)

Loan sharks, of course, were just this side of the tracks from Mythological Status in the Universe.

Legend from Melvinge's home burgoid would have it that loan sharks came from the Flatbush System in the Brooklyn Galaxy. They tended to be big, they tended to wear leather jackets, and they all tended to be named Louie or Butch, Bad Muvva or Sdark (the latter being, of course, Flatbush-speak for "Cute Little Axe Killer").

Loan sharks, Melvinge had read, had early on discovered that for some reason their home planet had a plentitude of mint trees. Nor was this mint foliage the source for leaves involved with the making of mint juleps or after-dinner mints or Franklin Mints (Brother of Benjamin Mints). No, they were paper money mints and they somehow magically grew the legal tender of all the civilizations in the galaxy.

Now at first the loan sharks, whose appetite for alien flesh was enormous, enjoyed great feasts of the thousands of foolish souls who came to get all that money on the loan shark planet. However, pretty soon folks wised up and stayed away. After all, you couldn't spend money, even if you had a whole bunch, if you were dead.

However, by this time the loan sharks had a taste for juicy, meaty, otherworldly meat, most particularly of the humanoid variety. At first they lured unsuspecting beings to their world with classified advertisements reading FREE MONEY and COME TO THE PLANET WHERE MONEY GROWS ON TREES and WHEEL OF BIG BUCKS—WIN FABULOUS PRIZES. However, soon enough word got around that creatures venturing to the Flatbush area of the galaxy ended up as featured items in loan shark corner-deli displays.

Their source of fresh meat depleted, their appetites still strong, the loan sharks decided to venture out onto the Interstate. For some years they declared themselves converted to vegetarianism and carried mammoth tumblers of V-8 to prove their point. Not only did the loan sharks essentially bankroll the Megaverse Mall with their ample funds, they also allowed various entrepreneurs to borrow money to open up highway food stands. However, it soon developed that the loan sharks had a curious way of collecting on overdue payments.

If you owed them money, they ate you.

For this reason, they'd just as soon you owe them big bundles because they had plenty of money in all currencies and denominations anyway. What they didn't have was fresh meat and they were continually hungry for it.

Before long the UV organization (Universal Vegetarians) disowned them, but by this time it was too late.

They had their nasty, hungry fins into practically EVERYTHING.

Of course, where Melvinge came from was so far out of the normal stream of things that loan sharks seldom ventured there. People tended to be skinny there anyway—pretty slim pickings for drooling loan sharks.

So the news that they had been swallowed by one of these gigantic beasties was not exactly blissfully wonderful stuff to Melvinge and Harlan.

"I suggest that we take whatever measures necessary to extricate ourselves from this situation," said Harlan.

"I don't like the look of the controls."

Harlan raised his eyebrows. "They still look like controls to me."

"Yes, but notice the lights."

"What lights?"

"That's just it, Harlan. They're out."

"Meaning, I presume, that the power systems are out. But the Grab still speaks. And what about yours truly? I, after all, am a psychophysical emanation of the Grabovnikon."

"A pimple on my nose, Harlan," pronounced the Grab in supreme distaste.

"You see!" said Harlan, grabbing onto the voice's presence hopefully. "Grabovnikon! What's happened to the controls?"

"Primary power supply has been shorted out in the descent into the loan shark's stomach. Repair servos are at work on the problem. Meanwhile, I am operating on secondary power sources."

"Darn!" said Melvinge. "The Time, Space, and the Other generator operates on the primary power supply."

"So?" said Harlan.

"That's our only hope of getting out of this mess! I mean, we've got to warp/woof out before we get . . ." Melvinge gulped. "Digested."

"Oh."

Warp/woof was the technical term for creating an energy field around an object which produced a polystyrene reaction rather similar to nonstick cookware. The object with the field would slip from its time/space coordinates, do a double flip and a somersault, and then zoom through the Other like a bat out of Heck. This was easy. What was hard was guiding your vehicle to where you wanted to go and not ending up in the Mesozoic era as dinner in a pterodactyl nest.

Warp/woof was for obscure reasons also known as "barking the dog" and "catting the piano," though no one knew for certain exactly why.

"Well then," continued Harlan. "Pray tell, Grabovnikon. Just how long will these repair procedures take?"

"An hour and three minutes."

"And how long before we get digested?"

"The process of digestion inside a loan shark requires approximately a year," pronounced the Grab.

"Well, the chaps certainly savor their meals, don't they?"

"However, along about the eighth month, it's rather like a bad case of poison ivy—and in the ninth month, biological beings' skin begins dissolving."

Melvinge shuddered. "Well, we'll be out before then . . . I hope." Nonetheless, he felt a slight itching sensation.

He shook it off.

"Grab," he continued. "Once we get the warp/woof machines barking again—will we be able to get out of here?"

"Theoretically."

"Good, because that's what we're going to do."

"We've still got an hour to kill," said Harlan. "What do we do? Have a nice game of chess?"

"May I suggest that you explore the interior caverns of this creature," said the Grab. "There may well be some secrets to the universe here— as well as certain Fabulous Prizes from previous years."

"Maybe even a pair of squash shoes!" said Melvinge.

"Possibly. Loan sharks have a tremendous appetite and a great capacity and they swallow just about everything they possibly can. However, I strongly suggest you look for the creature's currency reserves. Unfortunately, we do not have a great deal of money in the Grabovnikon—something you neglected to procure for our visit to the Megaverse Mall, Melvinge—and something that we most definitely will need."

"Yes, quite," said Harlan, his eyes glittering at the thought of hard cold cash. "I always meant to talk to you about that, Mel. . . ."

"I just figured we'd earn it on the way. Or find it, somehow."

"And look, here's our opportunity. So what say we pop out of this place and take a look around. Who knows what we might find. Our fortune . . ."

"Or maybe big trouble."

" . . . or maybe Speckled Petunia muffins!" said Harlan, becoming absolutely whimsical with delight. "Or Juniper Juice Egg creams! Or maybe just millions and millions of greenbacks, smackeroos, gonzolas!"

"Huh?"

"Various sorts of currencies from different planets, dear boy!" He raced to the Grabovni-kon's closet rapturously, tossed back various articles of clothing, and selected a bright orange raincoat and two pairs of black Wellington galoshes.

"Here you go, dear boy! Apply these to your extremities. If we're going to be sloshing about in loan shark digestive juices, you're going to need some protection."

"Do I have to wear such a tasteless raincoat?"

"Tasteless? I'll have you know that I was given this as a present from the Queen of Beetle Grease herself!"

"Isn't that Betelgeuse, Harlan?"

Harlan made a dismissive gesture. "Oh, I don't know. It's something yucky, that's for sure."

"I don't know. We'd better check this out." He tilted his head to the Grab's audio receiver.

"Hey there, big guy. What kind of atmosphere have we got out there?"

There was a moment of silence, with a trace of the working of instruments. Click. Whir. *Clunk!*

"Clunk?" said Melvinge.

"Just trying to assimilate the carbon. Hard brittle stuff!" said the Grab in a serious voice. "Right! The atmosphere! One part strawberry cola, two parts Elizabeth Taylor's Passion Cologne (p.u. by the way), one part argon, three parts bargain, a little splash of toilet water, three parts digested human flesh (oh my!), and, oh yes, some hydrogen and oxygen. In short, it smells rather like a perfume show at a garbage dump!"

"Oh well, I've been on the New Jersey Turnpike!" said Harlan. "I can take *anything*! Tally ho!"

They went to the door, opened it.

Melvinge gasped as he saw what lay outside.

It was the most incredibly strange stuff he'd ever seen in his entire life!

Even stranger than what the Fat Men from Space poured on their potato pancakes.

Chapter Nine

Ratner's Tail

Love that Stellar jelly donut, love that
  Galactic Dessert;
But inside the Loan Shark's gut, it's just mushy
  dirt.
> —Blind Grapefruit

Unfortunately, due to important narrative reasons, the narrator must take his prerogative as Auctoral God and change the scene.

Besides, haven't you been wondering what's become of Ratner, anyway?

Actually, Ratner is still running very hard, puffing and huffing after the loan shark as it slithers away through the dessert bordering the highway. The man would surely not have been able to wade through the whipped cream and the chocolate sand—but Sdark the Loan Shark either laid everything flat or simply pulverized it, leaving a plain of mashed candy upon which Ratner could tread.

And look! He's reached the tail! Ratner is jumping! He's got it! He's holding onto a fencepost of a land barnacle! He's hauling himself in! A cow is mooing encouragement from a pile of straw!

He's *made* it!

The barnacle animals applaud wildly.

The reason for our digression from inside the loan shark, however, has much more to do with a reason to pause and relate exactly where Melvinge's father has been all this time, rather than to view this jump, albeit exciting. (And a very lucky accident! Thanks, Ratner! Bravo!)

Ratner had indeed headed out that fateful evening years before for the local Bowl-A-Rama, not only for a heaping bowl of delicious rama noodles (topped with ketchup), but for a relaxing game of lame duck pin (a pretty fowl game sometimes, one that his heckling wife thought was for the birds). However, he stopped into the Magic Russkie Tavern for a bowl of bonzo borscht (beets, plus a whole lot more) and that was his mistake. For the Magic Russkie Tavern was actually a polka-dot slave ship in disguise and poor Ratner was shanghaied!

When the captain of the slave ship realized that Ratner wasn't truly polka-dotted (he just had a bad breakout of acne that day, something that always happened when he ate bonzo borscht) it was too late to take him back. And they certainly couldn't take him to the Paisley Planet for duty in the Rice

Crispies mines. Paisley Planet folks only paid premium prices for polka-dotted creatures. It was their belief that one day the Gigantic Pencil in the sky would come down and connect all the dots on their polka-dotted slaves and the resulting message would be the Secret to an Eternal State of Cream Cheese, a kind of Dairy Nirvana.

Anyway, Pegleg Irving, the slaver captain, sold Ratner for loose change to a casino owner on the Really Ugly Cheap and Rotten Gambling Planet (also know as Las Venus). The casino owner wanted to use Ratner as a spittoon. However, as soon as Ratner was placed into a gambling hall, he convinced the casino overseer that he could deal a pretty mean game of "kip- per canasta," a particularly slippery form of "21" or "Blackjack" involving dead fish, mallets, and potato chips.

Soon Ratner was a big success on Las Venus, and not only as a dealer. Since he tended to sing as he crushed dead fish and potato chips with the mallet, his talent with tunes was soon discovered by Shifty Pete Furbomeister, the talent agent for half of Las Venus. Soon Ratner began singing at all the best bars—the Runes, the Suds, Pluto's Detox, and let's not forget the Pagan Paisley, where the petrified body of that famous singer Elvis Paisley stood in state, performing a tape-recorded version of "The Star-Spangled Banana."

Songs that Ratner sang included "The Yellow Bagel of Texas," "Stranglers in the Night," and "When You Knish Upon a Star." These he sang in a falsetto resembling that of another Las Venus lozenge singer, Fig Newton. Newton, not only a lozenge lizard (indeed, his nickname was "the cough-drop Kid") but a particularly litigious lozenge singer, sued poor Ratner for stealing his style and Ratner was placed in a '67 Volkswagen, pushed out upon the highway, and told to amscray and never come back.

Ratner had adventures hither and yon through the galaxy, through Time, Space, and the Other, serving for a while as elephant delouser for Hannibal; speech stool for Attila the Hun, Alexander the Great, and Napoleon; and hood ornament for Flash Gordon. This and all the Other adventures too tumorous to mention deserve an entire other book (and indeed may be mentioned when other Worthy and perhaps Unearthly Narrators take over this saga).

However, just *how ever* did Ratner end up at Pinkie's Chili Dog Stand? That and that alone is the relevant question and will be addressed (and stamped) herewith:

To wit:

Thusly:

After a particularly long stay upon The Planet With, Like, Really Great Root Beer Floats, serving as a soda jerk in a Magic Moocow diary store (where you write the day's events in

94

ice cream—a ceremony of great metaphorical import which most folks have long since forgotten the meaning of) Ratner could scoop a mean dish of vanilla and dash on sprinkles with the best of them. It didn't take long before he obtained his PhS (Pretty Hot Scooper) in Ice Cream Academia at the University of Maraschino Cherry Pits.

He decided to move along the Interstate to another Dairy University planet. There was a nice little Ivory Log college up in the Milky Way that had just the position for him and there was a possibility that he could get tenure in Rum Raisin studies.

However, Cosmic Fate has a way of missing the beat to the Dance of Destiny and stepping on mortal toes.

Ratner's Volkswagen was rear-ended by a runaway garbage truck on the East Passaic ramp of the Interstate. Ratner was thrown clear of the car—clear into a matzo ball factory where he was pummelled and thummelled by thousands of machines and then dumped into a gigantic vat of chicken soup. He certainly would have drowned but for the watchful eye of the kosher clerk who promptly dragged him out and gave him mouth-to-mouth regurgitation.

Ratner recovered and was fine (although he never could abide matzo ball soup again) except for one major problem.

He'd lost his memory.

The only thing he remembered was how to be a short-order cook or a soda jerk. That and the batting statistics for the Cleveland Indians in 1959.

This did not stand him in good stead with his goals:

A) Getting back home;
B) Finding the Megaverse Mall; or
C) Finding a good podiatrist to take care of the corns on his feet from all the walking he was doing.

However, he *did* manage to snag that job at Pinkie's after an extensive interview and on-the-job proof that he could deep fry a chili dog with the best of them.

And so he'd lingered there, a thoughtful amnesiac, reading copies of Malt Diznee comix (Malt was Walt Diznee's younger brother in the weird animal-entertaining food business), and cooking up chow like a demon.

Until, of course, the sight of his son Melvinge and that *annoying* dogoid Harlan jogged his memory back into place.

Now he was hanging from a barnacle fence post and his allergies were acting up!

Ratner was a strong, wiry sort, though, and was able to finally pull himself up and into the barnacle, making his way through the hay and straw (ah-choo!) and then on up the loan shark's sleek hide. He crawled from barnacle to barnacle (stopping briefly for a glass of chocolate milk from a Cocoa Cow) until he finally reached a gill slit.

At this point, Ratner stopped for a moment and asked himself, "Hey. Just *what* the heck am I doing?" The chocolate milk curdled in his stomach, and his innards seemed to billow up toward his jowls.

Just what *was* he doing, anyway?

Riding a loan shark?

This was absolutely certifiably *loony bin* stuff!

But then, he remembered Melvinge. Melvinge, his son. He recalled Melvinge's early days, when he would dandle the lad on his knee. Melvinge was the best dandling kid a guy could ever want. All the guys on the block would come 'round and say, "Gee, Ratner. I wish my kid could dandle like that."

Of course, Ratner was never quite sure exactly *what* dandling was—but Melvinge could certainly do it well!

Naturally, Melvinge was far too large to dandle now—but still, Ratner loved the kid.

He couldn't let his son stay inside the belly of a mean old loan shark. No sirree bob!

He didn't care squat for his invention, the Grabovnikon. He could just cobble together another one of those. And as for Harlan—well, that dogoid deserved a good swift kick! And Ratner was just the guy to send it, first class!

Decision made, Ratner took a deep breath.

"Tonto!" he cried.

But before he had a chance to correct the Indian name to accompany his plunge, he slipped on a bit of shark mucus and slid into the gaping gill cavity, down deep into the center of Sdark the Loan Shark.

Chapter Ten

The Incredible Adventures
of the Starship *Mortimer*

Time and again, I see da light.
Time in again, I feel da pain
Ain't nothin' like a Endorphomite.
Hope I don' see one 'dem again!
—Blind Grapefruit

Without a doubt, you are wondering this question:

Just what exactly is it that our heroes Melvinge and Harlan are staring at and so awestruck by?

What is it that's so weird and wonderful?

Well, we'll get to that bit eventually. First though, you've probably been wondering another question.

Namely, if Larry the Werewolf really bit Melvinge, and he's really become a werewolf too, how come he's practically bald now?

I'm glad you asked that question.

Actually, Melvinge's lack of body hair would indicate that the Grabovnikon had been going *away* from the Mall, rather than toward it, correct? However, with all the hubbub about getting the chili dog for Harlan, he'd quite forgotten all about this whole werewolf business.

He wouldn't be able to ignore it for long, because as it happened Sdark the Loan Shark was headed in the general direction of the Megaverse Mall. . . .

Indeed, if he hadn't been so overwhelmed by the sight before them, Melvinge might well have noticed that his shorts were getting a mite itchy.

"Good gozongas!" said Melvinge, scratching his posterior absently. "I don't believe it!"

"I *say*! Well now, isn't this odd," said Harlan, his usual blasé attitude blown away.

Before them stretched a series of what appeared to be film and television studios. In the opened studio before them were the sets and actors of nothing less than Melvinge's absolute stone favorite television show, *Star Warriors and Planet Cruisers: The Midget Squad.*

The *Midget Squad* were a group of little people aboard the S.O.S. *Accident*, a starship of the fictional "Amalgamation"—a group of planets devoted to the game of Bingo. It was the mission of the starship *Accident* to travel from planet to planet, bearing peace and enlightenment, bingo games and markers, and a weekly hygienic health message.

Melvinge's favorite episode was "Planet of the Mint Floss," whereas Harlan's was "The Horrendous Earwax Creature of the Outer Pleiades."

"Captain Crankcase!" gasped Melvinge with absolute delight. He jumped off into the digestive sludge and waded knee-high in his Wellingtons toward the scene of the filming. "Dada! There are a million things I have to tell you!"

Captain Crankcase was the executive officer of the starship *Accident*. Dada was his robot first mate, a being who looked like a botched attempt at modern art. There were other members of the crew of the starship *Accident* of course—Fred the Klingfree Underwear Man, Miss Lollipop the Canadian Candy vendor, and of course the ladies' favorite, Bruce, who not only had a pointy nose and chin and muscles but an extremely repressed IQ.

Melvinge had always wanted to go to a *Planet Cruisers* convention in which fans of the show dressed up as their favorite hygienic devices; however, he'd never had the chance.

Now they actually had the chance to get on the Sacred Set of the Show! Melvinge had heard that *Planet Cruisers* was filmed in a mobile studio, but he'd never imagined that it would be inside of a loan shark!

Now if Melvinge and Harlan had not been so enraptured by the sight of the set of their

101

favorite TV show, they would have had the time to notice that the interior of the loan shark had a veritable smorgasbord of interesting items on the walls, all smorgasbordering a gigantic lake of bubbling digestive fluids.

This was the loan shark's "collection," and now he owned the Grabovnikon as well, (although the Time, Space, and the Other machine had yet to be properly catalogued by the bacterioid creatures wiggling and hobbling around on the catwalks on the periphery. No, the Grab lay dead in the middle of the lake amongst other flotsam, jetsam, and spam).

"Ugh!" said Harlan. "Oh my goodness."

"What's wrong?" said Melvinge, annoyed to be distracted from the magnificent vision before him.

"It would appear that I have stepped upon a head!"

Melvinge looked. Sure enough, it *was* a head. Sid's head. It floated in the water like some rotten apple defying a game of bobbing.

"Actually," the head said when they looked down, "I'm not really Sid's head. I'm just a growth."

"Oh, dear," said Harlan. He grimaced and distastefully booted the growth out of the way.

They forged onward to the television set, ignoring the sheen of engines and plumbing, the glow of doubloons, pearls, and precious gems glimmering like rainbow moss upon the sides of the loan shark's stomach.

No, no. Something far more important lay ahead.

The bridge of the starship *Accident*!

"What the devil is that blasted commotion out there!" cried the director. He spun on his heel, jodhpurs aswish, his beret nearly hurled from his head, and dark glasses sparkling in the arc light like the heart of diamonds.

The actors on the bridge of the starship *Accident* all swivelled away from character to glare at the new arrivals who had so rudely interrupted the progress of this important scene.

Melvinge was mortified.

However, Harlan, evermore the bold talker anyway, struck forward opportunistically.

"Well then! Hello there! I am the dogoid Harlan. And this is my boy . . . I mean my friend, Melvinge. You have to forgive Melvinge. He's a rabid fan of your show."

"Well, who isn't?" said the man. He sashayed forward, and it was only then that he saw a flash of the infamous purple hair.

It was none other than Fritz Spitz, creator, producer, director, writer, designer, and janitor for the most popular silly-science show of all Time, Space, and perhaps even the Other!

Silly-science, of course, was that branch of fiction with space ships, monsters, brave adventurers, and commercials for tooth polish.

It was not only Melvinge's favorite form of reading material, it made great liner for the numerous bird cages in his mom's aviary.

Melvinge supposed that the most winning aspect of *Planet Cruisers* was that, what with all the hullabaloo crowding about the Interstate, it was the one place where nothing much ever happened.

This, perhaps, was the genius of Fritz Spitz. Instead of trying to imitate the frenetic pace of life in the hurly burley vortexing about the Megaverse Mall, he had a group of odd characters that the common man could identify with. Whole shows were spent on the subject of the application of underarm deodorant, say, or the controversial use of Odor-Eaters in Dada's space-boots (which led to frantic battles amongst the fanatical "Cruise-nodes"—fans of the show—as to whether or not Dada the robot's feet stank).

In one particularly violent show, the starship *Accident* was invaded by a group of mutant cockroaches who proceeded to infest Captain Crankshaft's comix collection. The entire show was spent in heated argument with the Intergalactic Orkin man as to whether or not the captain's complete run of the *Incredible Hulk* comix could be saved.

The ratings were low. The show was far too exciting. The story editors were immediately fired and replaced by more suitable recruits from an Institution for the Mentally Moribund.

Ratings immediately increased and then, in a brilliant move, Spitz produced a show about toilet etiquette and cleanliness on a starship, simultaneously releasing colorful, sanitary toilet seat covers featuring pictures of members of the famous crew.

The marketing company was soon flush with sales.

"*Planet Cruisers* is the most popular show in the galaxy," continued Spitz, completely unmindful of the rude narrative interruptions. "It defines the arc of current civilization."

"Wow. So nice to meet you," said Melvinge, totally awestruck and looking around his body for a pencil and paper for autographs.

"One question, however," said Harlan, rocking back on the heels of his shoes (a quite difficult task in Wellingtons in the midst of digestive juices atop the highly spongy inside surface of a loan shark stomach). "If Dada is such a smart robot, how come he can't dot the letter 'i' in his sentences?"

Spitz sniffed arrogantly. "Characterization, dear boy. A flaw, if you will, in his otherwise sterling robotic self."

This was, of course, of absolutely no importance to Melvinge, who jumped up with glee onto the set and started getting autographs.

"See here!" cried Spitz, slapping a riding crop onto his jodhpurs in a commanding fashion.

"You're interrupting our shoot. And of an important scene! Captain Crankshaft has just discovered a planet with a cure for baldness!"

Melvinge was overjoyed.

"Wonderful! Marvelous!" he cried.

However, little did he realize it, but Sdark the Loan Shark had covered a great deal of mileage in the dessert and had drawn much closer to the Megaverse Mall than ever before—which precipitated a certain unpleasant side-effect in Melvinge.

He begun to turn into a werewolf.

It started, as these things usually do, with the hair.

Melvinge grew it.

Lots of it.

He grew it out his ears, he grew it out his nose. The hair curled out from his shirt and sleeves like bushels of wheat. It *exploded* from his cheeks like face spaghetti. It even grew out of his shoes.

Then the fangs. The fangs grew out of his mouth like tusks. Slather and drool began gushing and his eyes grew fierce and red. He stooped over on all fours.

A fearsome-looking beast indeed! But inside, of course, there was still the ever-sweet Melvinge . . . a Melvinge viewing this change not without alarm and perhaps even a little horror.

Those darn gypsies! That blasted Larry!

However, when he tried to explain to the assembled cast of the starship *Accident* that he was still the ever-sweet Melvinge, and not some fierce throat-ripping fiend, the explanation came out as a fierce roar and a feral snarl that frightened them all (Melvinge included).

The cast ran for cover.

Spitz, however, steeled himself and continued filming. "Great!" he said. "We can use you for a beast from Aldebaran! It'll save us thousands of samolas in makeup costs!"

However, just in the midst of the unexpected, the even more unexpected occurred.

Sliding down the slippery esophagus and plopping down right into their midst came none other than Melvinge's father.

Ratner!

Chapter Eleven

The Downside of Upittyness

Now I seen some trouble, 'fact I seen a lot.
  I seen catastrophes to make a man cringe.
But I tell you, believe it or not.
  Ain't nothing much worse than what happened
  to Melvinge!
                                    —Blind Grapefruit

There are legends in the Megaverse. Wonderful tales of great heroes of olden days of yore. Heroes with long flaxen locks who rode upon mighty chargers and brandished huge broadswords and rescued damsels in Distress, New Jersey.

Melvinge had read these stories—all of them—and he idolized these heroes.

His absolute favorite was the story of Ogoth Pectoral, mighty champion of the Greasy Empire in the Bronx Age (right before the more cultured and witty Irony Age). Ogoth was part human, part god, and part guacamole dip. (Enid Hammerhead, *The Doom Avocado and Other Vegetable Gods,* 1951.) Although his greenish tinge marked him off from other heroes of his time, and he tended to leave a greasy mayonnaise ring in the bathtub, Ogoth was an exemplary exponent of the heroic mythological archetype. (Translation: He had muscles the size of watermelons, mowed down bad guys like a Toro, made curvaceous cuties drool, and wasted monsters with his broadsword.)

However, of all the heroes, in all the legend, in all the lore of all the lands of all the galaxies in all the universes from the depths to the backside of Time itself, Ogoth Pectoral was unique in one respect.

Ogoth Pectoral was a *mensch*.

He was a real nice guy.

He was the kind of hero that heroines could take home to their parents for tea and cookies. He was the kind of hero that would stop one of his quite difficult labors and contests (brick-hod carrying, Parthenon building, gyro-eating contests, feta cheese throwing) to get a pet hydra out of a tree or walk an old medusa across a busy intersection.

Legend had it that Ogoth was *such* a nice guy that when he wasted a baddie, he actually coughed up the pennies for the dead guy's eyes so he'd have fare for the ferry ride down on Mickey Charon's boat to the mythical underworld, Diznee Hell. (Governed by the dog-god Pluto of course.)

All his life, Ogoth had been Melvinge's idol.

Melvinge wanted to *be* Ogoth Pectoral.

He didn't have the watermelon muscles and he didn't have the flaxen curls and he didn't have the broadsword and he wasn't part God and there wasn't a *speck* of guacamole dip in his entire being (although he'd once made himself sick trying to eat a whole bowl of the stuff).

But he was human and he did good things.

And he tried to be a *mensch*.

He tried to be a nice guy.

The only good thing about this whole were-wolf *mishigosh*, in fact, was that Melvinge could relate it to an Ogoth story.

"Ogoth and the Wolfman," appropriately enough.

It would seem that in his youth, Ogoth Pectoral was a great fan of horror movies. Now, this might seem a bit anachronistic to classical scholars, but one must accept the fact that the lands along the Interstate were much closer to Classic Comix and perhaps even closer to "Calvin and Hobbes." Anyway, take my word for it, in Ogoth's book, nothing was much better than lugging a couple of huge shopping bags of buttered popcorn down a dark aisle of the Acropolis Bijou and plopping down into a soft chair for the Midnight Creature Feature.

Ogoth loved Boris Karloff, he adored Bela Lugosi, and he would have run the Marathon with a cow on his back to see any movie with Vincent Price, Christopher Lee, or Peter Cushing.

But Ogoth's absolute favorite film actor was the incomparable Lon Chaney, Jr. Sure the guy was kinda ugly, and he couldn't act too well, and he only appeared in grade Z movies—but hey, who else could have played the Wolfman like Lon Chaney, Jr., huh?

Anyway, needless to say, Ogoth's favorite film was *The Wolfman*. The one with Bela Lugosi as the gypsy? A Universal treat.

Well, as it happened, while Ogoth was watching this very movie the guy in front of him turned around and who should it be but a werewolf? The werewolf bit Ogoth on his big toe and then wisely skedaddled.

Ogoth started growing excess body hair almost immediately. This was very unsettling, since he was due to get married next month to the Goddess of Fat, Diameter. Diameter said she wouldn't get hitched to him with all that hair sticking out of his tux, so he'd better do something about it, fast.

Ogoth went to an electrologist, but he was absolutely shocked by the prices.

So he decided to try to get the solution to his problem from his old friend, Sally Sphinx. Sal was a great old gal and a lot of fun at parties (especially when she found suckers who couldn't answer that hoary old "four-legs, two-legs, three-legs" gag and got to eat them!), and she knew just about everything. The only problem was that she tended to talk in riddles—

and to get the answer to anything, you had to solve them.

"Goth old pal, you look a bit hairy there. What happened?" she said to Ogoth as he schlepped up wolfily to her.

Ogoth explained the situation and wanted to know if Sally Sphinx had any solutions, fully expecting the "Riddle me this" line.

Instead, she said, "Nope."

He blinked. "Sally. Don't let me down. You know everything. Surely you know *something* to do in this absolutely itchy situation!"

"Short of a silver bullet in the gourd, buddy— no, I don't."

This did not sit well with Ogoth. For, after all, even a nice guy gets cranky sometimes. He unsheathed his broadsword and got—well, a little threatening.

"C'mon, Sal. I feel like fireants are having a barbecue on my body! Gimme a break or I'm gonna have to whack you!"

"Goodness, Ogoth. You don't have to get uppity here! Okay, okay. Actually, I think a man's a lot more masculine with a little nostril hair— but maybe I see your point. Okay, I'll give you the riddle, but you're not going to like it."

Riddle? *Now* they were talking turkey with garlic on it!

"Shoot!"

"In the 1961 film, *The Raven*, featuring Boris Karloff, Vincent Price, and Peter Lorre—what

113

caused Lorre to become a flapping creature of the night?"

That was simple. "A magician's spell."

"Right. Well that's what you're going to need to do the presto chango, buddy."

"But I don't *know* any magicians!"

"I can get you a magician, pal. Just put that broadsword away. Nothing spooks a magician faster than a bare, gleaming broadsword. Do you realize how high the wizard fatality statistics are in ratio to barbarians with broadswords? A dog in the middle of a freeway has a better chance of survival."

"Okay." So Ogoth hid his broadsword behind a bush while Sally Sphinx summoned the wizard.

Well, what the wizard did was a whole different story that might well be related in some later chapter of this Pinkwatery saga.

However, the significant aspect of the Ogoth tale for Melvinge (no, we haven't forgotten Melvinge) was that when Sally Sphinx uttered that incantation, the wizard *fell from the sky*.

Much as Ratner fell from the esophagus vent in the stomach vent, straight into the midst of the *Planet Cruisers* set.

It could well be understood that Melvinge viewed this as something of a miracle. He took one look at the fallen Ratner, and this time he *recognized* the man.

"Father!" cried Melvinge.

"Uhmmmmph! Groan!" said Ratner, much the worse for wear for all the running and jumping and falling he'd been up to lately.

"Ratner!" said Harlan, not entirely pleased at this abrupt entry. (Harlan and Ratner had been known to have disagreements before.)

"Good grief! Will there never be an end to this stream of interruptions?" said Spitz. Then he looked at his camera and realized that it had been on all the while, filming the abrupt entry of Ratner. "Hmm!" he said thoughtfully. "I suppose I might have a use for this footage! Entrance: STAGE UP!"

Ratner, finally finding words, spluttered up, goggling his son with great joy.

"Melvinge! Son!"

There was a wonderful reunion.

Not a dry eye in the house.

In fact, (sniff), pardon me, but your narrator (sniff sniff, HONK!) needs a break to recover from the waves of sentiment pouring from this story.

Tear-jerking stuff, huh?

Chapter Twelve

Gypsy Violence!

Oh baby! Sing those blues
  I wanna hear you yowl and howl.
'Cause Melvinge is doing that werewolf rag
  deep down in a loan shark's bowel!
                              —Blind Grapefruit

There. That's much better. Uh huh. Where were we? Oh yes, of course, the reunion of father and son and dogoid on the set of the most popular television show filmed in the digestive system of a loan shark.

"Son," said Ratner, patting his boy on the back. "You've grown so much! And you've grown so much hair! But you are my boy, I'd recognize you anywhere!"

Melvinge recounted the misadventure involving Larry the Werewolf and the gypsies.

"Yep," said Ratner. "Gotta watch out for those gypsies. The fortunes they tell are usually *bad*."

"It's been a long time, Father!" said Melvinge, wiping a tear from his eye.

"Pardon me, son—but exactly how long?"

"Well, sir—I was seven when you got lost on your trip to the Bowl-A-Rama. I'm seventeen years old now, almost eighteen—so I guess that means it's been ten years!"

"You always did excel at math, Melvinge!" yapped Harlan tartly.

"Harlan!" said Ratner. "As irascible as ever! I should never have whelped you from the Grabovnikon. Biggest mistake of my life!"

"Oh!" Harlan said, rolling his big brown dogoid eyes skyward. "Ten years of peace and enjoyment, destroyed! Oh, the revenge of the chili dog! We never should have stopped at that godforsaken place!"

"Hmm!" said Spitz. "I don't think we can use this particular stretch of film." He turned off the camera. "Too bad, really. Rather touching! Oh well. You really must excuse me. I must go off and round up my cast and crew. We've got another show to finish!"

And with that, the genius tottered off.

The reunion continued. Past years were recounted. More hugs were exchanged.

Then, just in the midst of a rousing tale from Ratner concerning a particularly harrowing escape from the Bagel Factory of Death (he'd almost been drowned in a vat of poppy seeds) a sonorous voice wafted across the lake of digestive juices.

"Ahoy!" bellowed the Grabovnikon. "I do

118

believe that my facilities are powered up properly. You may board and utilize the Time, Space, and the Other engines when ready!"

"I'm not so sure!" said Harlan. "How can the Time, Space, and the Other field get us out of *here?*"

"Yes, Father," said Melvinge, scratching his hairy neck uncomfortably. "You made those engines. You know how they work. *Can* they get us out of here?"

Ratner coughed. He coughed again, harder. He coughed so hard that Melvinge felt compelled to whack him on the back. But of course Melvinge remembered now that coughing was perfectly okay.

Coughing was what Ratner did when he was thinking food-o-scientifically.

Finally, after his recovery from this particular paroxysm of whooping-thought, Ratner held a finger up into the air.

Melvinge could almost see the light bulb appear above Ratner's head.

"Yes! It will be difficult, but I think I know a way to rearrange the pretzel-circuits to create a corollary snack-food field that will resonate against the roast-beef neurons of this fella's own operational equipment. Let us go! There is no time to waste!" He paused and looked at his son. "By the way, have you got any chips and dip on the Grab, Melvinge? I'm *starved!*"

*   *   *

The radical theories of food-o-science were developed by a former nurse-novel writer named Lafitte Conn Cupboard while hawking cheap slice-and-dice appliances on independent globular television.

Food-o-science took regular science by the scruff of the neck, stuffed it into a blender, and turned the knob to "Puree." The result was a marvelously gloppy way of looking at the very building blocks of matter, the very substance of Time, the very texture of Space, the very calorie content of the Other.

Food-o-science ignored "silly-science" concepts like atoms with their electrons, protons, and neutrinos. It simply scoffed at all the excessive rigmarole of quantum mechanics and mathematics and all that Newtonian and Einsteinian high physics nonsense.

The universe, said food-o-science, was like a kitchen, with a refrigerator, food cabinets, cookie jars, spice cabinets, and of course a big bread box.

All you had to do to accomplish anything different in the universe, maintained Lafitte Conn Cupboard, was to act like you were creating a new recipe for lunch or dinner.

And of course, to do this, you needed the patented Cupboard mental kitchen appliances, bestowed upon lucky food-o-scientists on spare weekends. All this involved was a metaphorical lobotomy—but hey! Lose a little, gain a lot.

When you were finished with the course in Lafitte Conn Cupboard's *Psycho-Dynamics,* you had all the wonderful Inner Kitchen technology you needed to cook up a mess of neat stuff like Grabovnikons!

It was with this powerful mental scientific technology that Ratner went to work on the pretzel circuitry of the Grab, while noshing on barbecued potato chips and French onion dip.

"You see, son!" said Ratner, pointing to the galvatronic creampuff distributor connected by licorice whip wires to the baked ham shaft. "All you have to do is to know the basic tenets of food-o-science, and you're a Master of the Megaverse! Voila! An Eternal Indigestion Engine!" With that, he changed the Wesson oil, put some holy water in the praydiator, and checked the carbohydrate-ator.

Then he made them both sandwiches, sat back, and regarded his handiwork. "Ah, yes, son. The wonders of food-o-science! And all you have to do is to send away for your weekly lesson. A mere $19.95 a month. Less if you send in the coupon!"

"Father," said Melvinge, chomping down his sandwich with one bite. "What exactly is an Eternal Indigestion Engine? And what is it going to do to get us out of this loan shark?"

"I'm glad you asked me that, son," said Ratner. "It's really very simple. You, of course, are aware of the principles behind this engine's precedent, the Internal Combustion Engine?"

"Yeah, you mean the sort of engines that make the sacred 1957 Edsels run?"

"Quite. And bless their holy manifolds! Well, as you know, in an Internal Combustion Machine the gas goes to the piston chambers where it gets blown up, propelling pistons which turn the crankshaft which make the wheels go round and round and makes the Edsel *go!*"

"Yeah!"

"Good. Well, using the food-o-science metaphorical exchange principles, what happens with an Eternal Indigestion engine is that it uses the 'gas' from the decomposing food—" Ratner belched and smiled. "—to power 'Energy Pistons' which align with any powerful energy source nearby, bond with it, and cause it to serve as a kind of cosmic crankshaft!"

"You mean . . ." Melvinge's eyes filled with awe and wonder.

"Yes. We will be using the Time, Space, and the Other engines of the Grabovnikon to link with the Time, Space, and the Other machines of the loan shark. Thus, we will drive him—"

"Like a 1957 Edsel!"

"That's right!"

"Weren't Edsels a 1959 car?" said Harlan, just to be contrary.

"Oh, details, details! You know what I mean,"

said Ratner, throwing the dogoid a hambone just to shut him up.

"But, Father," said Melvinge, a little confused. "If we do that . . . where will we take the loan shark?"

"To a cannery, hopefully," said Harlan, mouth full of hambone. "Pack him in tins as tuna fish and get us *out* of here!"

"I said shut up!" Ratner sniffed, burped, and continued. "No, Melvinge. Don't you understand? This is your opportunity. No . . . this is *our* opportunity."

"Opportunity? Opportunity for *what*, Father?"

"Opportunity to get to the absolute pinnacle, the tippy top, the crest of the hill, the pretty peak! Why son . . . the true end of all quests, of course! The Megaverse Mall!"

A thrill shot down Melvinge's hairy spine.

The Megaverse Mall!

Finally!

But the question remained: were a new pair of squash shoes really worth all this hassle?

It worked.

Ratner's food-o-science doctoring had turned the engines of the Grabovnikon into a splendid example of ingenuity on the half-shell with cocktail sauce and crackers.

"Engage!" said Ratner.

And when the engines engaged and produced

the necessary field, Ratner was able to use the controls to align it with Sdark the Loan Shark's Time, Space, and the Other machines.

Sdark, moving blissfully by now through the dessert, digesting his meals, watching reruns of his favorite show *Planet Cruisers* (which was why he'd swallowed the cast, crew, and creator to say nothing of the sets—he wanted his own creative input!) was suddenly catapulted, bellowing, into the Other.

Confused, alarmed, cursing, the mighty beast struggled, but to no avail. Something had control of his drive engines, and that something was hurling him into the mysterious mists of the Other (a place he rather disliked since the many creatures he'd killed tended to live there. It was thus a place where Sdark the Loan Shark was not particularly popular, and where therefore he had to move very, very carefully lest he bump into personages even more deadly, if not quite so large, as himself).

Through the subcortical interstices of the very essence of Thought/Flux/Energy/Nestle's Chocolate Drink streamed the loan shark, bearing in its gut our heroes. Through the very intertwining dances and prances of the Interstate ramps it ghost-barrelled, churning through the very soft nougat center of Life/the Universe/and Hoboken, New Jersey, itself!

Then, however, quite suddenly it took an unexpected detour—so unexpected that all the ambulatory members of the Grabovnikon were hurled from their ambules . . . I mean, their legs.

"What's going on?" cried Melvinge. He was rather ambivalent about this whole business. While it was nice to think that they were going to make it to the Megaverse Mall, the closer they got, the hairier he became.

"MMMMphhh! Murummmph!" said Harlan. The hambone he'd been enjoying had managed to get lodged in his throat.

"I'm not really sure!" said Ratner, worriedly examining the dials and controls of the vehicle. "I can't—Wait a minute! There's some sort of nether force—it's sucking us down into a gravitational pinworm hole! I can't seem to get a tab on exactly what's causing it, but whatever it is, it sure ain't good, let me tell you that, bud!"

Abruptly the Grabovnikon lurched again.

"Going down," said the Grab in a worried voice. "Going *way* dowwwwwnnnnnnnnnnnnn . . !"

The Grabovnikon spun tail-lights over antennas, skittering down into a chasm of darkness, and all its members lost consciousness.

When Melvinge came to, the first thing he noticed was the burnt ham-and-pretzel smell of the short-circuited engines of the Grabovnikon.

"Argh! What was the number of that side of beef!" said Ratner, clearly quite alive.

"MMMMmpphh! MMMMMMMphhh!" said Harlan, also alive and still having problems with that hambone.

Seeing that his companions were A-OK, and also noticing that the door of the Grabovnikon hung ajar, Melvinge went to explore.

He poked his head out and was immediately sorry he'd done so.

"Hello, there, furball!" said Novaleen the Gypsy Queen. She held up a collection of little dolls atop a model of the Grabovnikon. Gypsy voodoo! "Told you we'd be seeing you again!"

Larry the Werewolf pulled out his Smith & Wesson .45 and shot Melvinge dead with a silver bullet.

Chapter Thirteen

Death Is Just a Silly Melody

Dem bones, dem bones, dem wet and wild dancing
   bones!
Poor Melvinge! He got the Death Blues,
Do *you*, Mr. Jones!
                                    —Blind Grapefruit

   P.S. Hang around there, guys, for a real
      scameo!
   I'll give you a hint! I make a cameo! (B.G.)

Melvinge had never given Death a great deal
of thought. It was just what happened when
you were about a hundred and one years
old and things got real boring. Since he was
only a teenager, he'd figured he had a while
to go.

So when that silver bullet zapped through
him and he keeled over like a concrete bagel,
he was more than a bit astonished.

The most astonishing thing however was that
even though he was dead (he knew this because
he wasn't breathing anymore and he didn't feel
a pulse or any other sign of life in himself),
he could still see and hear what was going on
around him.

Was this part of being a dead werewolf?

If so it wasn't bad . . . not bad at all. Of course, not being able to move much had its drawbacks. But, somehow, Death had leant him use of his mouth.

So he said, "Ouch."

Down there on the ground, stone-cold dead, he still was able to say "Ouch" . . . which Melvinge thought was quite an accomplishment, for being *dead!*

Novaleen the Gypsy Queen meanwhile was giving Larry the Werewolf heck.

"Larry!" she screeched. "What did you do that for!"

"Look! I've changed my mind! This tribe doesn't need another werewolf, okay! I'm the werewolf! Take that earring back! That's how you trailed them . . . that and your gypsy curses. But now you've found them. Let's just be off, okay? I want a piece of raw meat pizza at that stand at the Megaverse Mall you keep talking about. Okay?"

No slacker, Snake-Spit had already sprinted up to prise the earring from Melvinge's ear.

However, Novaleen's withering screech stopped him midsnatch. "Snake-Spit! You murderous cur! Do not touch *anything* until you have my permission!"

"Yes, madam," Snake-Spit hissed, clearly not pleased by this reprimand but living with it.

"Now then, Larry. I'm pleased that your jealousy has showed itself. But gypsies can always use two werewolves. Especially if one is a *zombie werewolf!*"

A zombie werewolf?

Was that what Melvinge was now?

Well, that was okay, wasn't it? He could kind of lumber around all hairy and scary. When he was a kid he'd seen that Pittsburgh movie by Claudius Romeo, *Night of the Dead Lumbering Ugly People*. Scary! He'd always wondered what it would be like.

Still, even at this notification, he was finding it very hard to stand up.

"I can't stand up," he said.

"Take off the shackles, Snake-Spit!" commanded Novaleen.

So that was why he couldn't stand.

There, in that black-time when he'd gone down, a silver bullet with his name on it roaring through his chest (he could read it now, there laying on the ground: MELVINGE, in cute little letters), Snake-Spit had been able to come up and put some chains on his feet.

The shackles clanked away.

Melvinge stood up. A little shakily, true, but he indeed stood up, looking around despite the gaping bullet hole in his chest.

"There you go," said Novaleen. "You see! A zombie werewolf! Much better any day, I say, than a mummy werewolf!" She turned back to Melvinge. "You won't be able to stand up much, though, Melvinge. People are going to have to

129

drag you around a lot, I'm afraid. But that's the way it goes."

"But . . . does this mean," said Melvinge, choking a little bit with emotion, "that when I get to the Megaverse Mall . . . I won't . . . I won't be able to dance?"

Since we have not yet brought this topic up for discussion, that move might be propitious at this time.

The current most popular religion of the Mall, so say parking lot rumors, is Marathon Dancing—particularly jitterbugging.

This, in truth, is why Melvinge wanted those new squash shoes. Not for playing any silly racquet sports—oh no. He simply found them to be hands-down absolutely tops in the marathon dancing department—and that was what Melvinge ultimately wanted to do when he reached the Megaverse Mall. His plan was to gain power and recognition (and maybe get a few dates) by winning dance contests throughout the parking lot. Rumor had it that if you had enough wins by the time you reached the One True Mall, you got to be in the Finals.

And if you won, you not only got to visit the Megaverse Mall—

You got to actually *live* in the Mall!

Melvinge had become a competent hoofer by watching *Member of the Wedding* at least fifty or sixty times one week when he had the flu. One of the things that he needed to win these dance contests at the Mall, though, was a partner.

But how could he find a partner now that he was a zombie werewolf? He wouldn't be able to dance now, anyway!

Sigh.

O woe was Melvinge!

"Oh dear," said Harlan. He'd finally gotten the hambone out of his mouth and was venturing out to see what was happening.

"Melvinge, you don't look so good."

"Son!" cried Ratner. "What have they done to you?"

"That's okay, Father," said Melvinge. "I'm only dead. Look, I think I still do a mean soft shoe, though." He put one foot (paw?) out in front of the other in an attempt to execute a fancy dance step.

However, instead of making like Gene Kelly or Fred Astaire or perhaps a slow-motion Michael Jackson, he merely lumbered.

Lumbered along, out of control, past the gypsies, past Larry (who made a botched attempt at grabbing the earring) and straight into the arms of a Gypsy Princess named Loola, who was just coming out of her caravan to see what all the hubbub was about.

"My goodness. A zombie werewolf," said Loola, blinking dark, mysterious, mascaraed eyes. "And he's really cute too. What are you trying to do, Mr. Werewolf?"

"The name is Melvinge," said Melvinge, looking up dumbstruck. "I'm trying to dance!"

Melvinge was looking up dumbstruck for a very simple reason. This Gypsy Princess was absolutely drop-dead, pinch-me-I-think-I'm-dreaming gorgeous! She had long dark hair, tied with a colorful gypsy scarf, and she wore a bright purple blouse with puffed red sleeves. And lovely black dancing shoes.

"Dance!" said Loola, the lovely Gypsy Princess. "I love to dance!"

In fact, this was quite true, for Loola had been dancing to gypsy violins as well as gypsy rock 'n' roll since she was just a little tyke.

Loola! Lovely Loola! What a gal!

Blind Grapefruit sings a lot about Loola. Loola broke Blind Grapefruit's heart. Just by looking at her, his heart was broken—such was the effect of her beauty: even blind men could see Loola the Gypsy Princess.

Loola was born in Yonkers system, daughter to an itinerant peanut butter salesmen. Loola left her family to join the Tingling Brothers circus at the age of ten. In the circus she danced with the Jitterbugging Gypies. She was kidnapped by these self-same gypsies— and was sold to Gypsy Queen Novaleen to be their resident Gypsy Princess. This she did with flying colors, often to the point where Novaleen grew quite jealous of all the attention paid to Loola.

Still, Novaleen now had a wagon full of blue ribbons from the dancing contests that their princess had won.

Loola's motto was: "Gotta sing, gotta dance, gotta eat beans with rice!" The latter part of the motto, of course, was Loola's secret for health, stamina, and inner gas inflation—so vital in keeping light on one's toes!

However, although she had had dancing partners before, quite proficient partners as a matter of fact, none had really caught her fancy. None had that inner light she craved so much.

But this zombie werewolf named Melvinge did!

She could see it, flickering in his dead eyes.

Oh sure, he couldn't dance right now. But he was trying, that was the main thing. Besides, zombie werewolves could be cured of their problems. There had to be some gypsy cure—there were certainly enough gypsy curses, that was for sure!

"I'm so embarrassed," said Melvinge. His big chance, blown.

"Oh, don't be. I understand." Loola looked up to Melvinge, flashing the Morse Code of Love with her dark eyes. "Novaleen! This is truly ridiculous. Free this poor fellow of his curse! Let him sing! Let him dance!"

"But he makes such a fine zombie werewolf!"

"Look, I'm the werewolf here," said Larry, suddenly standing up on his two back feet and being assertive. "I don't need any competition."

"You'll do your job?" hissed Snake-Spit, doubtful.

"I'll do a darned good job too! I will terrorize the parking lot! The gypsy tribe of Novaleen will be feared and respected from here to the Mall itself!"

"Sounds good." Novaleen nodded. "He's kind of a lousy werewolf anyway. Okay. But I want my special earring back! That's why we've been chasing them. That's why I cast this gypsy curse to bring them to this place."

"Oh yeah, my earring!" said Melvinge. "Sure."

"Don't!" cried Harlan. "Don't, Melvinge!"

"Why?"

"Because it goes so well with your fur!"

"What a ridiculous creature!" said Loola, charmed and amused, but also a little annoyed at the brash attitude of this curious dogoid. "And what an odd vehicle. But no matter, Melvinge. Just take off that earring, hand it over like a good boy to Queen Novaleen, and then we can go dancing into the sunset! By the way, do you do the Watusi?"

It seemed so simple. Just unclamp this stupid earring (it had been giving Melvinge an earring-ache all book), fork it over to the Gypsy Queen and she'd cure him!

Only it wasn't simple, of course.

Because if it was simple, this wouldn't be the first book of a series.

PLOT COMPLICATION ALERT!
PLOT COMPLICATION ALERT!

For who should choose to appear at that very moment, flying straight in from the Other, his dark glasses shining, his blues guitar strumming, mouth harp gleaming, but none other than that old bluesman, Blind Grapefruit himself!

"Don't give that earring over to this wicked gypsy!" he hollered, shaking his guitar and generally carrying on, stompin' mad. "She don't know what it is, you don't know what it is—but I know what it is and—" The old bluesman suddenly stopped mid-rant, his old scuffed jeans aswish around his shoes, his torn jacket disheveled. He adjusted his threadbare hat, twitched his nose. His ear seemed to grow larger, and if Melvinge didn't know for certain that Blind Grapefruit really and truly was *blind*, then he could have sworn that B.G. was *looking* dead at him (so to speak).

"My lord, son!" said the old bluesman. "You been changed to a zombie werewolf! Bad juju!"

"That's right," said Melvinge. "But Novaleen and Loola assure me that if I give them the carring cvcrything will be hunky dory and I will continue on my way to the Megaverse Mall!"

"Ain't necessarily so, boy!" said Blind Grapefruit. "Besides, let me tell you all! Like I say, that ain't no ordinary earring! That be none other than the Earring of Erk!"

"The Earring of Erk!" cried everyone in unison.

For everyone knew what the Earring of Erk was!

Chapter Fourteen

The Earring of Erk
—or—
Lobe of My Life

Let me tell you now son, about the Earring
  of Erk
And how everyone who wants it turns into a
  Jerk.

—Blind Grapefruit

The Earring of Erk, legend had it, was forged
of platinum, opals, sapphires, and Sweet Tarts
on the Planet Ping Pong.

It was a gift of a mighty Emperor—a fat little
toad-faced dwarf named Al—to his spectacular-
ly beautiful wife, Fern.

Now, this in itself is of no great concern. After
all, husbands give their wives earrings all the
time. Usually for birthdays or anniversaries
or Christmas or Mother's Day—earrings are
kind of generic gift, like ties or handkerchiefs
or Denubian casaba melons.

However, as it happened, the Sweet Tarts
in the mix were no ordinary Sweet Tarts, but
magical Sweet Tarts—and all guava flavored
to boot (yum!). Now as everyone along the

Interstate knows (but of which more provincial areas like Earth are ignorant), magical Sweet Tarts aren't really magical. Nothing is actually magical in the Megaverse. As author C. Clerk of our own planet once pointed out: "In an advanced civilization, everyday things beyond us will look either magical or out of a really keen Sears and Roebuck catalogue."

Actually, the guava Sweet Tarts were pulverized bits of corn syrup, sugar, and a very rare element called Burpidium. Burpidium, essentially, is a molecule containing huge rogue electrons, mostly all psychotic. These electrons rove their turf wearing leather jackets and chains, carrying switchblades, occasionally venturing out in packs to terrorize neighboring atoms.

When sufficient numbers of these molecules are banded together, this upsets the very fabric of the neighboring time and space (and plays heck with real estate values)—causing all kinds of possible rifts in Reality (and Realty).

What King Al had commissioned from his sorcerers was an earring that would subtly shift his wife's view of him, making him look quite tall and handsome to her. But the sorcerers involved were rather klutzy and placed far too much of the wrong kind of stuff in the jewelry mix—namely, too much Burpidium. The result was an earring that shifted the very nature of the Reality it was adjacent to—but only on the second Thursday of each month. As there were no Thursdays on the planet Ping Pong, the earring was no problem. However, when an interdimensional thief popped onto Ping Pong, appropriated the earring, and then headed straight for Thursday world—a planet where every *day* was Thursday—things got confusing.

The Reality Police had to be called in from their home planet of Phildick to straighten things out—but then when they got the alligators out of the trees and the sky out of the sea and the pizza out of the punch bowls and Dan Quayle out of public office, they discovered, to their extreme chagrin, that the Magical Earring was gone.

It had simply disappeared.

As many things that disappear often do, the Magical Earring ended up with the gypsies. But the gypsies, not very much in touch with Reality anyway, thought the earring had something to do with garlic and violins and curses and werewolves (of course, in the gypsy world *everything* had to do with garlic and violins and curses and werewolves and, oh, goulash . . . don't forget goulash, with lots of paprika!). So when Novaleen and crew got a hold of it, naturally they made it their Werewolf Earring (Snake-Spit wanted it to be the Goulash Earring, but Loola wisely pointed out that it would be kind of hard to chew).

And so they travelled with it along the Interstate and amidst the parking lot, somehow avoiding second Thursdays of each month (not very difficult along the Interstate where sometimes calendars get confused), and not realizing the wild card treasure beneath their very noses—I mean, *ears*.

But enough of a pause for explanation.

Let's get back to the story.

Blind Grapefruit has the stage.

"That's right," said the old bluesman. "The Earring of Erk! Now that means, boy, that you get to make any wish you want to—because the Earring of Erk will grant it."

"But it's not Thursday!" said Magda Novaleen.

"It is now!" said Blind Grapefruit.

Sure enough, Melvinge could hear one of the gypsy grandfather clocks begin to toll the hour of midnight.

The day had changed.

And indeed, it must have changed to Thursday, because everything else began to change then, too.

Being familiar with the Interstate and the parking lot makes one prepared for the unusual. All sorts of strange sorts drop in and out for vaguely comedic purposes, and reality is always a bit fuzzy.

However, as already pointed out, the Interstate looks pretty much like the New Jersey Turnpike with lots of comfort stations, so Melvinge and company had a fairly reasonable grip on what things were supposed to look like.

So it was a bit of shock when the whole marsh/petrochemical factory/concrete ramp-and-snack-bar panorama began to *shift* and *distort* and generally look like a bunch of seasick funhouse mirrors on an ocean liner. Colors swirled like little Joey's fingerpaints dumped into a draining bathtub. The parking lot shook, but not like an earthquake—more like they were on Plastic Man's stomach in the midst of a particularly violent contortion.

The pots upon the cooking fires at the gypsy camp sloshed over, spilling soup and goulash everywhere. The atmosphere reeked of garlic and paprika—and then, much more.

It seemed as though the entire stew of the Universe was pouring into the area. Tea pots and plumbers helpers. 1970 Dodge Darts collided with German U-boats. Fredrick the Great was doing the breast stroke in a fish bowl while an admiring Queen Victoria looked on while chatting with Mao Tse Tung.

The gypsies hit the ground. Larry the Werewolf covered his eyes and whimpered. Ratner and Harlan scrambled back into the safer, saner hold of the Grabovnikon.

It was all just *too weird!*

Even *TOO WEIRD FOR A DANIEL PINK-WATER BOOK!*

It was certainly too much for Melvinge's brain to take. His mind began to boggle. And a boggled mind is not a pretty sight, take my word for it. It felt as though the gray matter were leaking out of his ears!

"Melvinge!" cried Blind Grapefruit. "Hurry! The Earring of Erk's powers are running unchecked. Its holder must act to contain it!"

"But what do I do?" cried Melvinge over a wind that howled above. Looking up, he saw a tornado. And in that tornado were none other than Sdark the Loan Shark, Sid, and his diner.

They all crash-landed noisily about fifty yards away.

"Make a wish!" Blind Grapefruit said. "You've got to control the powers by making a wish!"

A wish?

Melvinge didn't know what to wish for. The thing he'd really wanted most of all, he realized, was to find his missing father . . . and Ratner had found *him!*

The other thing that he wanted a lot, of course, was to get to the Megaverse Mall.

The problem with that was that if he went to the Mall like this, he wouldn't have much fun. Not as a zombie werewolf.

So that was what it had to be then.

"I wish I wasn't a zombie werewolf anymore!" he cried.

Suddenly, it was as though someone had pulled the plug of the movie projector showing this mess.

Everything not only stopped—all the craziness disappeared. Except for Sdark the Loan Shark, Sid, and the diner, everything just evaporated. The boring old parking lot was the boring old parking lot again, Juicy Fruit wrappers, Big Mac packages, and crunched-up Coke cans and all.

And Melvinge wasn't hairy anymore. He didn't have fangs. He was back to his cute baby-face self.

He was no longer a zombie, either.

Unfortunately, however, there was one little problem.

"There's one little problem," said Blind Grapefruit, looking down at Melvinge as he lay on the ground.

"What's that?" said Melvinge.

"Yeah! What's the problem?" said the feisty Ratner, tearing out of the Grabovnikon, ready for action.

Harlan poked his head out, a little more cautious.

The gypsies, however, had had enough. They were packing up to go. They'd had enough of this crazy Melvinge guy! Only Loola was staying.

She'd decided that Melvinge was just her kind of dance partner.

"Problem?" she said.

"What problem?" echoed Ratner.

Blind Grapefruit sighed.

"Well, sonny boy. You done cured the werewolf curse. And you ain't no zombie no more."

"Yes."

"But ain't you noticed one little detail?"

"What's that?"

"You can't move!"

Melvinge thought about this. He tried to get up off his back. He couldn't do it.

"Hey! You're right! What the! . . ."

"What's the problem boy?" said Blind Grapefruit sorrowfully. "Melvinge, you forgot to make the full wish! Hon, you *still dead!*"

Ratner waved this off. "A minor detail. You're still my kid, Melvinge."

"And I still want to dance with you! We'll work something out," said Loola, looking on the bright side of things. "I'll just strap you to me! Even dead I can just tell you're a better dancer than all the other guys.

"But what about the Earring of Erk."

"Only one wish per Thursday, pal," said Blind Grapefruit. "I kin tell I'll be singin' the Dead Melvinge Blues for a while."

"So don't worry about it, kid," said Ratner. "Come on, Harlan. Give me a hand and we'll carry him back to the Grabovnikon! It's the

Megaverse Mall or bust!"

"Let's just not hold our breaths, guys," said Harlan, and together they all carried the inert, dead Melvinge back to the Grabovnikon.

It was a kind of embarrassing way to end the first leg of the Quest for the One True Mall. Dead!

All in all, Melvinge thought, he'd rather be on Philadelphia World.

THUS ENDS THE FIRST VOLUME OF
MELVINGE OF THE MEGAVERSE.
DON'T WORRY ABOUT CRUNCHING
THIS BOOK AND ITS SEQUELS.
CRUNCH ALL YOU WANT.
WE'LL MAKE MORE!

Afterword

How many years ago was it, and why did I agree to it, and what was it I did? Moreover, is there any reason I should remember—or want to?

At the age of eleven I came across that passage in which Doctor Watson is astonished to learn that Sherlock Holmes has not even a rudimentary grasp of the principles of astronomy. Holmes dismisses the entire subject by telling Watson that as far as it applies to his area of specialization it makes no difference whether the Earth revolves around the Sun or whether the Sun revolves around Holmes's sitting room. He goes on to say that he regards the human mind as capable of holding a finite amount of random information, and that he chooses not to clutter his mind with facts of no immediate use.

I seized upon this rationalization and made it my own. Ever since, I have been more than willing to forget anything and everything, having made the assumption that one will automatically remember the really important stuff.

Applying this assumption to the present case, it does not matter why I agreed to this experiment, this literature in a petrie dish, this mélange, this witch's brew of a story. That I did agree is memorialized in a contract, a copy of which is in my possession, and the articles of which I am bound to observe.

The idea was for me to provide an appropriate assortment of dead body parts which would be stitched together and somehow animated by others. We all know what happened to Dr. Frankenstein, so maybe it wasn't an experiment—but what was it?

As far as I am able to tell from the heavily edited, condensed, and refurbished document which has evolved from that which I handed in, my original intention must have been to create a schematic of my long contemplated and never undertaken homage to Herman Melville, *Ishmael, or The White Novelist*. This is a story I had never actually tried to write, like so many of my greatest works.

This, the first book of the series, is for all I know a careful observation of the set of guidelines I provided. Or it's nothing like it. As I say, it's been years, and I don't remember why I did it, let alone what I did.

I *do* remember that not so many years ago in the ancient and historic city of Galveston, I knew a lambent wench by the name of Tanya—not her real name, but as Tanya the Chiropractor she gave transient relief to many a dockwalloper and roustabout in those happy days when a Polish sausage cost a quarter, and a doss for the night was the last refuge of scoundrels.

I had shown Tanya a kindness—cleaning out the raingutters on the quaint little house by the side of the road where she was wont to dwell. This common decency, which I would have shown a cat, had a profound effect on Tanya's soiled but capacious heart, and she would hear of nothing but that she give me all her earnings, cook me brimming pots of Brazilian *Fehjuajo*, and attire me in splendid suits in all the colors of a roll of Lifesavers.

Out of a deep sense of moral obligation to my fellow humans, the result of seeing a cartoon biography of Fyodor Dostoyevsky one cold November day, I stayed on in Galveston, clad in my suits of many colors, smoking cheroots and playing klaviash with other similarly situated young men. I did this so as not to give offense to

149

Tanya, and not because I enjoyed this indolent life. Indeed, the very figure of my New England Yankee being was inflamed at having no work to do.

Tanya had a cunning little boy, Nipper by name. She planned to apprentice the boy to a whaler when he was old enough to be of interest. I became a second father to this lad. (His natural parent, I was given to believe, had been the evil old Bischoff of Birmingham.) Many was the time when the adorable little moppet would clamber onto my knee and lisp, "Hey Mister, for a dollar, I'll take you to a dog fight," or some such endearment.

I took it upon myself to be a mentor to the snot-nosed little dripper, and taught him how to palm a trey, keep a knife in his sock, and many another innocent trick to gladden a boy's heart.

"I want to be just like you, bub," little Nipper, whose real name was David, used to say, while we shared a frosty mug of scuppernong on an afternoon, while his mother was busy doing good works. It was as close as I have ever come to paternal feeling. And not all that close, now I come to think of it.

In time, the boy was signed on the S.S. *Venus* as a cabin boy and began the career his mother had chosen for him. The tyke had early literary aspirations, and had already written a work for the stage, dedicated to Tanya, and entitled, *'Tis a Pity She's a Chiropractor*. He was obsessive about this fledgling drama, and tended to go on about it boringly. His mother worried that he'd make himself a nuisance aboard ship, and her parting advice to him was, "Little David, don't harp on your play."

David promised his mother he would not go on about his play to the discomfiture of the tars, saying, "I'd never consider an ocean voyage without taking this drama mine."

As the *Venus* backed out of the slip, and the distinctive figurehead disappeared from view in the Galveston Harbor miasma, Tanya shed a tear for the yob she might never see again, and sobbed, "To think that any son of mine would grow up to be a thespian!" Then she spat in the greasy water, and left to converse with a couple of sailors.

In time, Tanya contracted tendonitis and was sent to a sanitorium in the mountains. I waited around Galveston for a couple of days, and then hopped a freight train for Poughkeepsie with the intention of breaking into the literary life. I confess I forgot about Tanya and David in the metropolis, dazzled as I was by new associations with the local intelligentsia, the availability of two Dunkin' Donuts outlets, both of them open twenty-four hours, and the well-known aesthetic and cultural distractions of the home of Vassar College and Smith Brothers Cough Drops.

In later years, I heard that Tanya had recovered her health, abandoned her former life, and had snuffed it as a result of an industrial tragedy in a pyrotechnics manufactory south of the border where she had found employment as a Roman candle stuffer. Snuffed was the stuffer. Sic Transit.

Nothing was known of the fate of David, the little son of the Bischoff.

My own fortunes are well known to all people of discernment and education—the best-sellers, the adulation of a grateful public, my role as advisor to heads of state and captains of industry, and my pride and joy, the model farm in the suburbs of Poughkeepsie, complete with the world's largest herd of domesticated wildebeests.

Equally well known was my subsequent fall from grace, the dark days of addiction to spiked banana-pineapple milkshakes, association with nefarious characters and international terrorists, and the many questionable deals I made in my insane desire to have money with which to continue my careening descent to the gutter.

Here I must pause to give praise to the Hon. Baba Shim Wallah Boo, whose disciple I became when all seemed darkest, and through the practice of whose unique Transinfernal Metameditation I was able to begin the long climb back to sanity, decency, and peace of mind. My loyal friends and readers will be gratified, I know, to learn that I am now free of those demons which once made of me "such an obnoxious loony," as my beloved master used to observe.

Speaking again of questionable deals made when my mind was beclouded by drugs and artificial fruit-flavor—one in particular, iron-clad through the machinations of devil-lawyers, of which I am forbidden to write or speak—looms darkly over me to this very day and moment. The sapient reader will understand that to which I allude.

And yet, even as I continue to make my slow ascent back to respectability, notwithstanding old debts which must be paid to publishing predators and cutpurses, there is the occasional moment of joy. Such a moment was occasioned by the realization that the author of the volume you, the reader, now hold in your hand, is one David Bischoff. Yes, the same adorable little moppet who hawked second-hand postcards in the streets of Galveston so many years ago has grown into a great man and literary wallah.

Tears came to my eyes as I read the first draft of this offering. Also a constriction of the throat, and a whistling noise from the bronchiae—such was my happiness.

I wish the reader no less.

—Daniel M. Pinkwater